A Heart to Love

A Heart to Love

Sandra Horton

RESOURCE *Publications* · Eugene, Oregon

A HEART TO LOVE

Resource Publications
An Imprint of Wipf and Stock Publishers
199 W. 8th Ave., Suite 3
Eugene, OR 97401

www.wipfandstock.com

PAPERBACK ISBN: 978-1-7252-7808-0
HARDCOVER ISBN: 978-1-7252-7809-7
EBOOK ISBN: 978-1-7252-7810-3

Manufactured in the U.S.A.   07/06/20

The Holy Bible, New International Version, NIV Copyright© 1973, 1978, 1984, 2011 by Biblica, Inc. Used by permission, All rights reserved worldwide.

A Heart to Love is a work of fiction. Where real people, events, establishments, organizations, or locales appear, they are used fictitiously. All other elements of the novel are drawn from the author's imagination.

To my husband, my true north
*Without you, finding the cottage and all the rest
would not have happened*

Part 1

Lost and Found

1

I have set before you life and death.

DEUT 30:19

GRABBING HER JACKET OFF the floor, Liselle Wintersted slammed the door behind her, not bothering to lock it. Nobody did in this tiny hamlet where her search had begun and today she was in a hurry to catch the ferry. She didn't want to miss the early run to Anderson Island.

The morning sun threaded the trees as she glanced back at the Tudor she had rented five months before. With an artist's eye she admired the lovely butter cream siding and cedar shake roof, a medieval-style turret at one end and towering juniper at the other that gave balance and symmetry to the home.

Closing her mother's house in Olympia and taking a leave of absence from work to relocate to Steilacoom had changed everything, the decision forcing her to deal with the painful detour that life had taken. Here she found she could breathe easier as time and memories sorted into *before* and *after*.

Before mother had included lengthy hospital stays and interminable doctors' visits, waking each morning to a feeling of dread of the unknown, her stomach tied in knots.

After mother had brought hopelessly sad days as each morning she rose to lay her requests before the Lord: "Guide me, Father," she prayed. "Rescue me from this emptiness."

It all seemed surreal, trying to avoid everyone and everything that reminded of Ellen, which had, of course, proved impossible for every day

Monica called. If Liselle failed to answer, she soon appeared at her door. Monica and her mother had been friends forever.

～

The weather had been warm the spring her mother died. Usually cold and drizzly in the Pacific Northwest, sometimes well into summer, Liselle had overdressed. As she knelt by the catafalque that held her mother's casket, perspiration beaded her forehead.

Visibly uncomfortable, her eyes strayed to her father's headstone: Henry "Hank" Wintersted. He died when she was three. Now a fresh loss and Ellen to be buried next to the father she couldn't remember.

Brunch remained at the home she and mother once shared. Best get on with it, Liselle decided, and blowing her nose, she drew a deep breath. Standing, her heel caught in the hem of her skirt and caught off balance, she wobbled on uneven ground, jerked her foot and heard the fabric shred.

Marching across dewy grass, emancipated cloth flapped against her shins as she strode past towering pines and a cadence drummed in her head. Alone . . . alone . . . it seemed to mock as a breeze lifted her hair and distant blue-tinged mountains stirred memories of hiking Crater Lake with mother.

Unlocking her car, it was then she noticed her grandparents clinging together with frail stick arms. She hastened to help them get settled in the back seat and starting the engine, glanced in the rearview mirror, wincing at their pale, drawn faces. She should have stayed with them on this long, hard day of burying their only child.

Biting her lip, she navigated the car to a street filled with cars and parked in the driveway; then helped Grandmother negotiate the sidewalk while Grandfather followed with their handbags.

All that week friends had hovered, cleaning, preparing meals while Liselle moved dazedly through selecting a coffin and mother's burial clothes: an apple green suit, a silk scarf to hide her baldness.

As they approached the house, muffled voices floated out the windows as lace curtains tried to escape on the warm breeze. Inside, with flowers and food covering every surface, Liselle pasted on a smile as her mother's best friend reached to hug her. Monica had stayed close the last month and offered to stay with Liselle the night Ellen passed.

Liselle returned Monica's hug and slipped past the other guests and up the stairs to the quiet of her room. Changing into sweats, she tossed the ruined skirt in a corner and pulled her hair into a ponytail.

In the dining room, everything seemed to move in slow motion as she perched on the arm of an upholstered chair and woodenly accepted hugs from Ellen's living, breathing friends. Their lives would go on with trips, parties and outings, none of which would ever again include her mother. At the thought, icy fingers of fear gripped her.

Ellen had lived life to the fullest; no one would argue with that. She just wanted to live longer. Was there ever a good time to say good-bye to one you loved? When the diagnosis had come they remained positive, determined to beat this cancer. Liselle had never believed her mother would die for Ellen practiced a healthy lifestyle. But in the end, the malignancy had moved quickly, decisively through their ordered lives to shake Liselle to her core. But mother had never stopped encouraging her. "Liselle," she had whispered near the end. "Don't be afraid to live your life!"

2

LISELLE JUMPED AT THE tap on her shoulder and glanced up into Grandfather's pale eyes now sunk in shadow. For the first time she noticed how loose the suit hung on his narrow frame.

He motioned her to follow him and shuffled to the den where Grandmother sat on the loveseat. She held out her hand to Liselle and pulled her down beside her, wiping her tear-filled eyes for the hundredth time that day.

Liselle slipped her arm around Grandmother as Grandfather closed the door and cleared his throat. "Your grandmother and I need to talk to you about your mother."

Liselle frowned. What could be so important that it needed discussing today?

"You know we had Ellen late in life." He swallowed. "But . . ."

Liselle zeroed in on his moving lips. ". . . She was not our natural born child."

What?! Grandfather's words seemed to hang in the air. Before she could respond, he raised his hand. "And no, she never knew. We had given up on having children until one day our family doctor called; a young girl in Steilacoom needed a quick adoption of her newborn. We went immediately, everything handled privately." He paused.

When he continued, his voice shook. "We never expected to outlive Ellen. Now, when we are gone, you will be alone. You must find her family, your family, if there is anyone to be found."

He reached into his vest pocket and pulled out a small envelope. "This is all we got from the birth mother." He placed the envelope in Liselle's lap as she sat with bowed head, color flooding her face.

"Please don't be upset with us," Grandmother began.

Taking a deep breath, her hands shaking, Liselle opened the envelope and a pendant slid out followed by a photograph.

"The picture is Ellen's mother," they explained. She had always felt secure in her grandparents' love, believing nothing could change that; now she struggled with the question that must be asked.

"Why didn't you tell my mother?"

Grandmother burst into tears as grandfather stood silently, a stricken look on his face. When neither answered her, Liselle stood and placed the items on a side table, then turned and fled the room.

Conversation stopped as mourners turned her way. With ponytail bouncing, she shoved open the screen door and cleared the steps in one leap; then sprinted for several blocks to the shores of Puget Sound where she watched the waves cut fleeting curls before they disappeared into the depths.

Drawing fresh air into her lungs, she felt lost, shattered and alone. On the day she had buried her mother her grandparents had unburied the most incredible secret. They were not her grandparents, not her birth family!

"How is it possible," she asked the deep, "that they kept this from us?" The waves tossed foamy bubbles at her feet before racing back across blue tinged sand to water's edge.

On impulse, she slipped off her sneakers and tied them together. Wading into the frigid water, tiny shells crunched beneath her feet as the last gleam of sun outlined the chalky clouds. Mother had called it the "silver lining". If she were here now she would tell Liselle to look for it, be positive. "But how, mom?" she asked out loud. "How do I do that without you?" The roar of the ocean greeted her as the water tugged at her ankles.

∼

Retracing her steps home, Monica met Liselle at the door.

"I'm okay," Liselle reassured with uplifted hand and regret swept as she realized someone else had taken her grandparents home. She should have done that; instead she had thought only of herself. "Forgive me, God," she breathed a flare prayer, "I need your help, please guide me."

Returning to the den, she retrieved the photo to study the woman with hair the same fiery color as hers and Ellen's. Before today she didn't exist. She didn't even know her name.

The pendant, in the shape of half a heart, had an E engraved along its jagged edge, for Ellen? She curved her fingers over the smooth metal. And where was its mate? Who was this phantom grandmother and why did she give Ellen away? And Ellen was gone.

With fresh determination Liselle fastened the chain around her neck and resolved to wear the pendant until the mystery was solved. "So help me, God," she said.

~

As she jogged to the ferry, her thoughts turned to Jackson. He no longer fit her world either. Having met at hospice a few weeks after his mother passed, he in a support group while she grappled with what was to come, at first she felt drawn to him. He seemed further along the path to recovery, yet remained silent about his experience. When Ellen died, he had disappeared. Liselle hadn't heard from him since, hadn't told him of her plans to leave. With nothing specific to finding her grandmother, she imagined he would criticize her decision.

Perhaps moving to Steilacoom made no sense, but in the process she had fallen in love with the picturesque community, taking a waitressing job at a quaint little restaurant decorated in a whaling motive. Nestled on the shores of Puget Sound, it was here that ferries made regular stops as she watched commuters arrive and depart for surrounding islands.

Soon one island had captured her fancy. Shrouded in mist and a short ferry ride away, Anderson Island sat in the middle of the Sound. Perhaps life on an island would create an additional layer between her and the pain that stalked, as she desperately sought to fill the hole left by mother.

Her boss Jana chuckled when she mentioned her idea. "Anderson Island is very private," she explained. "And outsiders usually not welcome!" But Liselle was determined and began to plan her visit.

~

As she arrived at the ferry, Liselle pulled the photo from her backpack to once again study this unknown grandmother, the oval face and high cheekbones reflecting her own. Feeling the mist in the air, she shuddered and swept her hair into a knot, tugging her collar higher. Fingering the silver heart beneath her sweater, she wondered if the other half would ever be found. "I'm relying on you, God, to go before me and prepare the way."

The ferry's horn interrupted her thoughts and a freight train wailed in the distance as the crossing guard began its descent. Skipping across the tracks she turned to watch the train roar past.

At the pier she purchased ticket and latte as passengers scurried for buses. Climbing the stairs to the deserted upper level, she chose a booth midway and watched the gulls dive into the roiling waves.

On the deck below two vehicles were boarding: a flatbed loaded with lumber and a silver van. The driver remained in his truck while the pleasingly plump woman exited the van and began walking toward the stairs. Moments later she reappeared balancing a tray with coffee and bagel.

Liselle offered a smile and she beamed back, her salt-and-pepper curls framing a friendly face. "Good morning, dear, do you mind if I join you?"

"Not at all," Liselle responded.

"Are you visiting someone?" she asked, easing into the seat opposite.

"No . . ." Liselle hesitated; then decided to confide in her. "Actually I'm thinking of moving to Anderson and want to look at rentals."

"Oh, my dear!" exclaimed the lady, flustered, "Where are my manners? I didn't even introduce myself."

"That's okay . . ."

"But it's not!" argued the lady. "Forgive me for being so rude, my name is Lucinda McGivens Vankosky. My Grandfather McGivens was one of the first to settle the island!"

"Really!" exclaimed Liselle.

"Yes," she picked up the story, loving the telling of it. "Our history goes way back! Grandfather was a ship's mate at the time they were searching for passage through the islands near Fidalgo and Whidbey." Liselle nodded, vaguely remembering those names.

"Anyway, Grandfather took a liking to Anderson, purchased land, married my grandmother and moved here after their house was built. My grandmother had red hair like you, not plain like mine. By the way, what did you say your name . . . ?"

"Oh," said Liselle, spellbound by her tale. "I-I-I guess I didn't. It's Liselle."

"Leez-ell," the woman repeated, rolling the name off her tongue. "I like it; it has a lilt to it. Now you call me Lucy, just plain ole Lucy, none of this Lucinda-stuff, and you must let me show you around."

"Thank you very much . . ." Liselle began.

"Oh, it will be lovely . . ." Lucy said.

". . . but I really can't put you out," Liselle interrupted.

"Oh nonsense!" said Lucy. "Islanders love visitors and you must tell me all about yourself. I love a good story! And I can't get over that hair, such a unique color."

"I guess it runs in the family, my mother was a redhead." Suddenly it felt odd to mention Ellen in the past tense and tears welled.

"Well, I had mousy hair before this salt-and-pepper," Lucy soothed.

"Your hair is distinguished," Liselle argued. "My mother never hid her gray and I thought it made her look mature and elegant."

"My husband said that, too. Now he's gone," Lucy lamented.

"I'm sorry about your husband." Liselle blinked back tears.

"Your mother sounds like good people," Lucy said, gently placing her hand over Liselle's. The ferry's engine slowed to a whine and they bumped against the pier as Liselle stood to collect their cups.

"Anderson Island, here we come!" Lucy said. "You must let me drive you around, then come to my home for lunch?"

"Yes, I'd like that, very much."

There was a warmth and openness to Lucy that immediately drew Liselle and she decided to enjoy the day with her before catching the ferry back.

3

PINE AND FIR SCENTED the island as Liselle powered down her window and breathed deeply. She caught glimpses of deer in the misty forest and gazing upwards, studied the glide of a red-tailed hawk through the trees.

Lucy circled south to Thompson Cove and Nisqually Reach, then west to Drayton Passage, Anderson Bay and Yoman Dock as she pointed out different homes. "This one is nice but may be too big; this smaller one has no windbreak. Most homes have wood-burning stoves."

It was obvious Lucy knew the area well as she recited its history. "The island was named after Alexander Anderson. He was in charge of Fort Nisqually in the 1800s, but Peter Puget actually mapped the Sound in the late 1700s if I remember correctly. The Native Americans were called "Chelakom" and these pink flowers . . ."

"Yes," Liselle responded.

"We call them chilacoom, or steilacoom."

Liselle felt a sense of peace in Lucy's gentle company; her fear of the future lessening. Perhaps living on Anderson would be good for her and she mulled it over, silently praying.

Mid-morning Lucy turned away from the water and drove up a one lane road that curved past a vine-covered church, its slim steeple dwarfed by towering pines. More pink flowers framed the arched windows.

"The church my grandparents built," Lucy said and Liselle craned her neck to study it. Continuing another hundred yards, Lucy pulled over and stopped the van, then turned to Liselle.

"Well, did you see anything you like?"

"I'm not sure," answered Liselle. "I think I'll know it when I see it, but maybe I should just pick something . . ." Her words were cut short as the sound of a truck downshifted behind them and both turned to watch the flatbed edge past with its load of lumber.

"I wonder where he's going!" exclaimed Lucy. "You don't suppose he plans to board up the old Wintersted house?"

Stunned to hear her family name on Lucy's lips, Liselle blushed but Lucy didn't notice as she continued. "It's the only house down here, has been deserted a long time. Sad, but I don't think anyone will ever live in it again."

Liselle could barely contain her excitement. "Let's follow him and see if you're right!"

"You're on! I love to snoop!" Lucy giggled as she swung the van back on the road. They caught the flatbed as it turned into the dirt driveway of a tiny weathered house, its whitewash long gone. Liselle stared at the cottage of faded boards as Lucy parked in the narrow drive. The workman ignored them and began removing plastic sheeting from the roof, a pallet of shingles on the ground beside him.

"It's a darling house," Liselle exclaimed as she stepped from the van and walked to the front stoop. Brushing past wildflowers, gingerly she stepped on rickety steps and walked across the decaying porch. Peeking in dirty windows, a Franklin stove stood on raised hearth in the front room, a small hooked rug beside it. Behind this room was a small kitchen with two-burner stove and icebox. Opposite were two smaller rooms and a tiny bathroom.

Liselle turned to inspect the yard. A gnarled apple tree cut a stark silhouette against the overcast sky while behind the cottage a jagged stream cut into the bank to create a swathe between house and forested hills as the stream continued to flow under a dilapidated shed supported on two stilts over the water.

Lucy showed little interest as she followed Liselle to the shed, the door creaking when it swung open. Inside rusty garden tools lay scattered among abandoned firewood and through missing floor planks they glimpsed the stream below.

"What happened to the people who lived here," Liselle asked.

"Hank and Lizzie Wintersted, I'll tell you over lunch," Lucy promised. "Right now it looks like we're in for more rain."

"Excuse me, sir," Lucy addressed the workman. "Are you repairing it?"

"Yeah, lady," he growled, shaking his head. "I don't know why it hasn't fallen down by now!"

The sudden downpour ended their conversation and in seconds they were drenched as they ran for the van. Lucy pulled towels from the back seat as she struggled to breathe. "My asthma," she explained.

Expertly maneuvering the van along the narrow roads, Lucy was soon turning down a lane lined with dogwoods to approach an imposing mansion with massive stonework across the front and light spilling from every window. With forest of Douglas fir behind and an expansive manicured lawn to welcome them, Liselle could only stare.

"It's lovely, Lucy, do you live here alone?"

"Yes and no," she responded. "It's just me and the help. I could never keep this by myself!"

She parked in the carriage-house and led the way along flagstone path where lilacs and roses mingled in sweet fragrance. "The carriage house was the original home," Lucy explained as they entered the kitchen through French doors. "I inherited this from grandmother, but it was held in trust until I was thirty. By then I was married and had lived here for ten years."

Wonderful aromas greeted Liselle as she almost stumbled into a young woman. "Cecelia my maid, she lives here," Lucy introduced and Liselle returned her shy smile.

"There's also my daytime help, Nyls the gardener and Emily my cook. You'll meet them later but first let's freshen up." Lucy guided her along softly lighted corridors as Liselle caught glimpses of rooms filled with lovely antiques and rich furnishings.

Lucy tended to the dramatic and now was no exception as she paused before a pair of ornately carved cherry doors. "This room is special, I hope you like it," Lucy said and with a flourish swung open the doors as Liselle giggled at her grand gesture.

"Thank you Lucy, I almost expected a drum roll . . ."

She stopped to stare at the exquisite Queen Anne furniture–she knew it from mother's design books–the crystal lamps and velvet wallpaper, a blazing fire that cast a glow over mahogany floors. In the center of the room, beneath coved ceiling was a four-poster bed with lace canopy, draped with a satin duvet in cream and rose.

As Liselle took it all in her eyes strayed to the Persian rug beside the bed; then stopped at the captain's trunk at its foot. The trunk, weathered and dented with worn leather hinges, seemed out of place in the room despite the crystal vase of freshly cut flowers on top.

Swallowing, Liselle whispered, "Lucy, you surely don't intend for me to use this room!"

"I knew you would like it," Lucy squealed. "This was grandmother's room . . . I've kept it just the way she did with flowers from the greenhouse. That's her portrait over the mantel."

Smiling, she added, "Why don't you change out of those wet things; you'll find a robe in the bathroom."

4

We are filled with the good things of your house.

PSALM 65:4B

Lucy closed the doors behind her and hummed happily to her room to change into dry clothes, then on to the kitchen to tell Emily of their lunch plans. She liked this nice, down-to-earth girl; what fun to watch her reaction to everything.

Somehow it seemed right that this girl with the fiery hair, so easily impressed, so vulnerable from the loss of her mother, should enjoy Grandmother's room. It was the finest in the house and filled with beautiful memories. Lucy loved to entertain, perhaps in that sense she was like Grandmother; God knows she didn't get her looks from her.

She busied herself in the kitchen stirring soup and slicing croissants, sending Nyls to the greenhouse for more flowers. If it weren't so rainy, she would go herself. Working in the earth, digging, planting, weeding, gave her a certain satisfaction that only her asthma kept her from enjoying more. Emily tried once to shoo her out of the kitchen, but Lucy wouldn't leave, happily anticipating an afternoon of telling more stories.

Liselle hesitated; she felt like an intruder in the elegant room, and tip-toeing across the mahogany floors, she stood before the portrait of the young woman in lacy white gown with blue sash. *Elizabeth* it said on the brass nameplate, her fiery hair cascading over creamy shoulders. She was dazzling.

15

Something about the picture seemed familiar and sliding the backpack from her shoulder, Liselle pulled out the photo. A chill went up her spine. There was a resemblance, her mother's eyes seeming to stare back at her.

"*Dear God*," she whispered, heart pounding as she considered the possibility and tucking her grandmother's photo away, she entered the bathroom and gazed out the window at a lone weeping willow that shaded a small pond. It reminded of the tree now shading her parents' graves. She and mother had planted it when she was six and all these years it had grown to now provide a place for her to grieve a life without parents.

She slipped out of her damp clothes and into the fleecy robe, wrapping its generous folds around her; then spread her sweater and jeans near the fire. Sitting on the bed, she brushed her hair by the firelight's glow.

With a light knock Lucy peeked in. "Hal-loo, are you ready . . ."

She stopped to study Liselle, damp tendrils clinging to her forehead, her length of hair cascading in soft curls around her face, and eyes that shone like sapphires in the firelight.

"Mercy, you gave me a start," Lucy exclaimed. "For a second you reminded of Grandmother." Shaking her head, she murmured, "It must be that hair!"

Quickly Liselle stood. "My clothes are still damp; may I come to lunch in this?"

"Of course, it's just us and the help today," Lucy replied.

In the dining room a blazing fire had dispelled the gloom, the table set with a steaming tureen of chowder and platters of fruit, nuts and cheese.

"Lucy, you shouldn't have gone to such trouble."

"Nonsense, I love to entertain, and besides, Emily did all of this."

Emily, her snowy hair piled on top her head and cornflower blue eyes twinkling, chimed from the doorway, "Yes, Miss Lucy loves to entertain, and she's a good cook too, don't let her fool you none!"

"Oh, go on now, Emily, you know I don't cook like you," beamed Lucy.

After a second helping of chowder Liselle sat back to admire the table service: Delft from Holland, Viennese crystal, English Spode, Belgium lace, gold Russian goblets.

"Forgive me, Lucy, I didn't realize how famished I was, your table service is incredible!"

"All came from Grandfather's travels." Lucy motioned to Emily to bring the crab and avocado croissants which they devoured in silence.

"Now," said Liselle, dabbing at crumbs with her lace napkin, "tell me about the Wintersted place."

Lucy clapped her hands in delight. "I love a good story, but the right story needs the right atmosphere; let's sit by the fire with our tea." She led the way to wing-backed chairs and matching ottomans in a rich floral print where they sank down comfortably with cozy throws.

"Let's see, the Wintersted place, there's a story there, not a very happy one, I'm afraid," Lucy began. "It all started many years ago right in this house."

"Here . . . Lucy, go on!"

Lucy needed no urging. "Grandmother had this young cook Lizzie who lived just down the road. Back then you understand everything was very, uh, primitive, no modern conveniences of any kind. The islanders farmed and fished. Of course my grandparents were well off, what with Grandfather being a captain.

"Anyway, Grandmother hired Lizzie Wilson to help. But times were hard and her parents had too many mouths to feed; soon they were telling Lizzie it was time to marry. But Lizzie wanted to teach, what future did she have if she married so young, her days filled with young'ins, cooking, cleaning, and mending, oh endless work. She was upset to see her dream die and of course she couldn't hide her feelings from Grandmother."

"What did your grandmother do?" asked Liselle.

"Captain–that's what everybody called Grandfather–he died right before this, so Grandmother offered Lizzie to stay with her, and Lizzie did, Grandmother being so respected in the community and all, what could her parents say. All went well for about a year and Lizzie continued to read the books in Grandmother's library. Soon a new face showed up, Hank Wintersted."

Liselle stopped sipping her tea.

"Apparently Lizzie's parents had picked a husband but he wasn't to Lizzie's liking. But Hank and Lizzie, now they were something. Lizzie lost her head over Hank and soon they wed. Hank was a first rate carpenter. That cute little cottage you saw, he built for Lizzie. A year or so later she gave birth to twin boys. Grandmother helped her afterwards since Lizzie's mother was keeping house over in Steilacoom. Times were hard, you understand."

Liselle nodded as Lucy continued.

"Grandmother had birthed my father by then, but it seemed like Lizzie filled some need for her, like maybe a daughter she never had. I don't know, it was almost like she was missing someone. I know that doesn't make sense, but that's what I heard. And sometimes I could sense it, too, especially when Grandmother tucked me in at night and read to me. Then she would get this far-away look in her eyes."

Liselle remained silent, her mind spinning.

"Now the part that's terribly sad is that Lizzie never liked that stream behind the house, you saw how it just kind of cuts through there?"

"Yes," answered Liselle. "I noticed that."

"Right, Lizzie never liked the stream 'cause little boys are drawn to water. She watched them like a hawk. They were about 18 months when Lizzie got news that her mother was ill. She couldn't very well take the boys, not knowing how sick her mother was, and Grandmother had gone to Seattle. So Hank took a few days off while Lizzie went to visit her mother.

"On the second afternoon, Hank was out front while he thought the boys were napping, but one of them got out the kitchen door. Hank found him about an hour later, floating face down wedged against a stilt under that shed.

"Hank was beside himself, Lizzie, too. They packed their things and left and nobody's lived there since. Oh, from time to time it may get rented out to summer visitors, but I don't think the Wintersteds ever came back. Not even to visit Grandmother . . ." Lucy's voice trailed off and they sat in silence.

A log snapped in the fireplace and they jumped. Liselle stood and walked to the window, her back to Lucy as she blinked back tears. This was a part of her father's life she had never known and she was deeply touched. She loved the little cottage her father had built.

Taking a deep breath, she spoke. "It's a sad story, Lucy, but before you told it to me I knew I wanted to rent the house. I still feel that way. Who do I see to make arrangements?"

If Lucy was surprised, for once she didn't show it. "I'm not sure. We can drive over and try to catch that workman. Maybe he knows."

Liselle raced to her room to change, thankful her clothes were dry. Grabbing jackets, they hurried to the carriage house and arrived at the cottage as the workman was packing away his tools, the porch repaired and new shingles on the roof.

"Excuse me, sir, we were here earlier," Lucy began.

"Yeah, I remember you," he nodded in Liselle's direction.

"We were wondering about renting this place, who to contact, who hired you to work here?" asked Lucy.

He laughed, an abrupt sputter coming from his throat. "Who hired me? I hired myself, unless of course you mean my father!"

"You're . . ." Lucy took a step back, ". . . you're the Wintersted twin?"

His face twisted from the painful reminder. "Yep, that's me, George the survivor." He turned away to continue loading his truck.

"I'm sorry," Lucy began. "My friend is looking for a place to rent. We didn't mean to upset you."

He shrugged, growled, "As you know, I'm not a twin anymore, except on this island . . . makes it hard to come here."

"I am sorry. Perhaps we shouldn't bother you," Lucy offered.

"I don't see why your friend here, sorry I didn't get your name . . . ?"

"Liselle."

". . . Lucille," he mispronounced, "can't rent the place. I'm sure she would take excellent care of it," he added.

"You wouldn't have to worry about a thing," Liselle said, noting the sarcasm in his voice.

"Well, you look like a regular sort," said George. "The rent is $100 a month and that's a good price on this island."

Liselle swung her backpack off her shoulder and pulled out cash for the first month. George pocketed the money and handed her the key which she slipped in her pocket.

Returning to the van, Lucy voiced her concern. "Liselle, are you sure you want something this old and small? It still looks kind of rickety, despite George's repairs."

"Yes, I know this is the place for me," Liselle explained.

"Well, you've missed the last ferry. Spend the night at my place and we can plan your move."

Liselle was overwhelmed by Lucy's generosity. "That sounds great and thank you, Lucy, for all you've done for me!"

The day had turned out quite differently from what she expected: the island tour and exquisite lunch, the special accommodations, finding her father's cottage. A great deal had happened, the added history of her father bringing him into clearer focus as mentally she created a space for him that had too long been empty.

~

Back at Lucy's, they retired to their rooms, Lucy with her latest mystery novel, Liselle in Grandmother's room curled up on the bed with old journals she had found on the bureau. Elizabeth's elegant script floated across the page with scenes of island life from long ago.

June 1, 1929

I traded the Cape Cod hens to Lizzie Wilson's dad . . . he to pay a dozen eggs each week for the next two months.

EM

5

THE NEXT MORNING LISELLE was up with the sun and dressing quickly. She had no idea where Lucy's bedroom was or how long she would sleep. To her delight, Lucy sat at kitchen table with coffee and newspaper. Upon seeing Liselle, she promptly put the paper aside. "Good morning, did you sleep well?"

"Yes, I'm excited about the move."

"Me, too," Lucy grinned, "Seems like the old Wintersted place will be an adventure. Now, how much stuff do you have? We can take the ferry over, drive the van to your door, load up and presto, we're back here with one load before lunch. Then we have the afternoon to get another load, what do you think?"

"One trip should get all my things," Liselle advised.

On the ferry over, Liselle barely noticed the gulls circling overhead to dive into the churning waves. She was torn over her decision to move, loved Steilacoom and the concerts at Pioneer Orchard Park, the salmon bakes at Sunnyside Beach. The most important thing now was to find her mother's family. She didn't want to live the rest of her life with questions. While the cottage promised a new angle on her father, so far she had learned nothing definite about mother.

She felt a deep sense of peace knowing that God had answered her prayers, bringing her and Lucy together. There was no other way to explain the timing or the sudden bloom of friendship between them. God had promised to take care of her. "A father to the fatherless is he," she repeated from memory.

Lucy and Liselle made several trips from house to van with clothing, books, cooking utensils, blankets and linens, an ancient oil lamp, cushions and crates of canned goods and cleaning supplies. Liselle supposed she should feel embarrassed at living with so few possessions, thought surely Lucy would say something, but Lucy showed great restraint.

With the last box loaded, Liselle paused in the turret room. The dreary day threatened more rain and the lovely house looked forlorn, even here where the light was best for painting.

A fresh canvas sat on the easel with slashes of red and black marring its white, the beginning of some expression and Liselle studied it before loosely wrapping it. She folded the easel and set it by the front door. "Goodbye, old friend," she whispered to the house as she gazed across the emptiness. "I will miss you."

The first of the month and her rent paid, she penned a 30 day notice to her landlord and placed it in the mailbox where she discovered a letter from Jackson that the post office had forwarded. Memories of their time together flitted through her mind. He was cute, but complicated, their budding relationship forced into second place when her mother's illness had suddenly redirected all her energy to survival. Now Jackson had resurfaced.

She stuffed the letter in her backpack and climbed into the van, "Let's stop for lunch where I work," she suggested to Lucy. "It's near the ferry."

"So, are you a cook?" asked Lucy.

"Oh no," said Liselle. "I wait tables. I like talking to people. No cooking for me, I wouldn't like being in the kitchen all day."

Liselle led the way to a booth in back and they sat in silence while the waitress served them lemonade and chicken salad, Lucy the epitome of politeness and restraint. "Lucy, I know you've got a million questions, and it's all right to ask them."

Lucy was thoughtful before she replied. "Not so much questions as curiosity. The way you live is different, maybe even scary to me. I've always been a consumer of fine things; everything planned out, including where I would live. Someone has always taken care of me: my parents, the trust, my husband, my life planned out neat as a pin. I am the keeper of the family heritage."

"I've really only been this unsettled since mother died," Liselle explained. "And I realize we do have a lot to learn about each other. Actually, I've been meaning to ask about the trunk in Grandmother's room. Do you know what's in it?"

"That old trunk . . ." Lucy chuckled, "I suppose it's filled with quilts and things. Why don't we take a look? And you must stay one more night;

you can't possibly want to move into that little place without getting some things from my attic."

"I really do have everything I need," Liselle began, but Lucy wouldn't hear of it. "This is my adventure, too," she said, "and I insist on being part of it."

Back on the island, they drove to the cottage, unpacked the cleaning supplies and went to work. When they were finished, the tiny house sparkled and Lucy had to admit it had a certain charm, though she shuddered to think of staying there.

With the last box unloaded, Liselle went to the shed for firewood and paused to gaze through the cracks at the water below. The little Wintersted boy was found there. She didn't even know his name. No wonder no one had ever re-routed the stream or moved the shed or fixed up the place. It was too melancholy to think about, too sad to be around. How her father must have ached for the rest of his life!

Yet knowing of his loss now gave her encouragement. He had kept going; she would too. Hank was part of her and she was part of him; how much faith it must have taken for him to continue on that path and sensing his strength, she felt a deep love for the father she never knew.

Collecting the firewood, she walked back to the house where Lucy sat on the front steps, breathing heavily. "Everything looks wonderful; I'm ready to go if you are."

"Yes," Lucy agreed. "George must have repaired these steps. Good thing or I would have fallen through!"

They chuckled as they climbed in the van and Liselle felt a sudden pang of remorse for not having explained that Hank was her father. Now it seemed awkward to bring it up and she wondered how to correct that. "Thanks for your help, Lucy. It seems I'm always thanking you."

"I'm glad to be of help."

"And Lucy," she continued, "However this adventure turns out I hope we'll always be friends."

"Why wouldn't we?" Lucy exclaimed. "I can't imagine why we wouldn't so just put the thought out of your head."

The weather drizzled all afternoon and they sat by the fire with mugs of hot chocolate. After dinner Lucy kept her promise to explore the trunk. Removing the vase of flowers and throwing open the lid, they discovered old photographs, souvenirs, and mementos.

"You didn't know these were here?" Liselle questioned as she pulled out a leather-bound photo album.

"Not on your life," Lucy responded, "I thought it was full of linens."

Liselle sat on the rug and, slouching against the bed, opened the album. On the first page was the same photo her grandparents had given her. "Elizabeth" it said on the back. Silently she absorbed every detail of the woman who was her grandmother before closing the book and sliding it under the bed, suddenly feeling guilty for keeping her interest in the cottage a secret.

She hadn't meant to hide her identity. Now it seemed awkward to reveal that Hank was her father. And Lucy had not asked her last name, an obvious oversight on her part, but how to correct that: Oh by the way, my name is Wintersted, what a coincidence! Only she knew that finding the cottage was anything but coincidence and in a flash she recalled how upset she had been at her grandparents for keeping her mother's adoption a secret.

As Liselle paced the room, Lucy was up to her shoulders in crocheted handkerchiefs and doilies. Suddenly she surfaced with a shout, clutching an ebony box, the initials EM on the lid. "What's this," Lucy gasped.

Liselle took the box from her outstretched hand, "Let's not explore anymore tonight, Lucy, we've done so much and I'm really tired."

"Well, sure, of course," Lucy agreed. "I didn't realize how late it is. Why don't we just push everything aside and in the morning we can put it back."

"I'm sorry . . ."

"I'll just clear a path and in the morning we can hit the attic, see what's up there," Lucy offered as she scurried around moving things.

"Thanks, Lucy."

"No problem," she replied, closing the door behind her.

$\approx$

Liselle climbed into bed without brushing her hair or teeth, worried that the box might be too personal. Another time perhaps, when she felt more confident about Lucy's reaction to her identity and what she suspected. Did she have enough proof that Elizabeth was her grandmother? That she was Ellen's birth mother?

She liked Lucy and didn't want to hurt her, yet she felt unsure that she had enough pieces to the puzzle. Lucy had a right to know, but how would she react? Would she be happy with the news?

Reaching into her backpack Liselle pulled out her Bible and fingered its soft leather cover. Mother had gifted it on her ninth birthday; it had since become her most treasured possession and over the next few years she had read her way through each book, like a pauper running her hands through gold, pleasing her family when she invited Jesus into her life as her Savior. Touching the pages, strong feelings stirred within. The words sparkled like diamonds for her, each one a promise from God.

Turning to the 104th Psalm she began to read: *"O Lord my God, you are great . . . the birds of the air nest by the waters; they sing among the branches . . . the moon marks off the seasons . . . how many are your works, O Lord, in wisdom you made them all . . . there is the sea, vast and spacious, teeming with creatures beyond number . . . there the ships go to and fro."*

The word "ships" jumped out at her . . . Captain and Elizabeth and everything they had labored for now here for her to enjoy. She thought of her own love of the sea, the walks on the beach that made her feel connected to the Creator. The ocean's sheer power and complexity always brought to her an overwhelming sense of awe and closing her bible, she fell asleep with it beside her on the pillow.

6

THE COOL BREEZES LULLED Liselle and she slept late. When she joined Lucy in the kitchen she expected to be teased. Instead concern etched Lucy's face. "Are you okay?"

"I'm fine, just a little tired after the last two days," she explained.

"I understand. If you don't feel like going up in the attic, that's okay."

"And miss an adventure? I think after breakfast I'll be raring to go!"

Lucy smiled at her enthusiasm. After devouring Emily's pancakes, they climbed the stairs to the attic where Lucy handed her an old scarf. "You'd better cover your hair, Miss Gorgeous. It's going to be dusty and filled with cobwebs. Whatever you want, just pile in the center and Nyls will load in the van."

As Lucy sorted through boxes at one end, Liselle started at the other and soon a stack had accumulated: a flower pot, lawn chair, bookshelf and small table, gardening tools, art supplies, horsehair chair, and whimsical wood carving of a boy and dog. When she asked about the carving, Lucy explained that Captain had whittled it when her father was a toddler.

Nyls made numerous trips back and forth from attic to van and finally they were off. At the cottage, it didn't take long to stack everything in the front room.

"Lemonade for everyone," Liselle announced. "And Lucy, you must sit, your face is quite flushed." She placed the lawn chair on the porch and Lucy groaned as she eased her weight into the webbed seat. Returning with small table and beverage tray, Liselle placed them next to Lucy and poured lemonade. "I know it's not as fine as your place, Lucy," she began, "but here's to my first guests."

"De-lighted" Lucy said as they raised their glasses and Nyls gave a quick nod of his head. While Lucy rambled with stories of neighbors, Liselle studied Nyls where he sat bent over his lemonade, floppy hat hiding his face. From the first day he had kept his distance, not friendly and welcoming like Cecilia and Emily. Just that quick nod when she tried to speak to him, almost as if he preferred not to be noticed. When she had queried Lucy about him, Lucy seemed not to know much. He was a loner, she said, had always worked for their estate.

"Oh, dear, look at the time," Lucy said. "We must be going. Are you sure you want to stay here tonight–alone?"

"Yes, I'll be fine," Liselle responded. "I have canned goods, plenty of firewood and the house seems quite sound since old George Wintersted fixed it up. I can't stay with you forever."

Placing the empty glasses on the tray, Liselle headed for the kitchen as Lucy followed carrying the small table. She turned to glance at Lucy and saw disappointment cloud her face. "Why don't you stop by mid-morning and see what else needs to be done," Liselle suggested.

"Okay, I'd like that!" Lucy's smile returned. "By the way," she picked up her keys and walked to the porch, "you never told me your last name."

"Oh," Liselle tried to sound casual as the door swung shut, "Its Wintersted . . ."

Shock registered on Lucy's face as the door closed and she almost dropped her keys as she tottered down the steps to her van, backed down the driveway and slowly drove home. Liselle was a Wintersted? How had she missed that?

Back at her mansion, sitting at the desk in her den, she wondered how Liselle's identity had not come up, especially after all their conversations about the Wintersteds. A flush colored her face. Had she been kind to Hank and Lizzie? She retired early after supper and a hot bath.

∾

Liselle was sorry that Lucy had discovered her identity that way. Though she had tried to act nonchalant, she knew her revelation had hit Lucy like a shockwave from Mount St. Helen's. Why hadn't she told Lucy when they first found the cottage?

Her mind in a whirl as she readied for bed in the place her father once lived in the house he had built she recalled bits of information. Hank was born in Washington but she didn't know he ever lived on this island. And while mother had mentioned George, they had never met, George bitter after his mother's death and his father remarrying, especially to a younger woman.

The fact that George didn't hear her name correctly and hadn't asked her last name had worked in her favor at the time for if Lucy had known her identity, as friendly as she was, she might have said something and George wouldn't have rented the cottage to her, not Hank's daughter.

Now she could only hope that Lucy wasn't upset for family and friends were the heart of Lucy's life and Liselle wanted to be a part of that heart. Wearily, she closed her eyes. The Lord gives and the Lord takes away— blessed be the name of the Lord, she breathed. "Good night, heavenly Father, please help Lucy understand and not be upset."

~

The next morning as Liselle brewed tea on the small stove, she remembered the cemetery near the church and pulling on knee-high boots– the meadow would be wet–and a hooded jacket, she headed out into the incredibly quiet morning.

A heavy fog blanketed the area and she set her pace to the rhythm of a favorite psalm, "*This is the day, this is the day that the Lord has made. I will rejoice, I will rejoice and be glad in it.*" As she walked, she felt like the only person in the peaceful silent world.

Near the cemetery the fog had lifted and she located the Wintersted graves first. There were three: a couple who had lived to old age, Hank's parents and her grandparents; a toddler of almost two, the twin who drowned. His name was Grant—George and Grant, her father's sons.

She moved on to the impressive "McGivens" monument. On the headstone was Elizabeth's name; below hers were Franklin and Meredith; Lucy's parents.

No one had groomed the cemetery for some time. Maybe in the spring she would come back and spruce it up. Kneeling now beside Elizabeth's monument she brushed away dried leaves to discover words etched in the granite. Catching her breath, she read the inscription:

I wish you enough loss to appreciate all you have.

Did the "loss" refer to Ellen? She wondered now if Elizabeth had ever told anyone about her baby girl.

"Strange," she thought, "no Captain on any headstone." She heard the whine of a car engine, stepped behind a tree and saw Lucy drive by. Deciding to circle back through the trees and approach her cottage from Oro Bay, she didn't want to explain her visit to the cemetery just yet.

As expected, Lucy was parked in her driveway.

"Hello, Liselle."

"Morning, Lucy, come in for coffee?"

"Okay," she agreed.

Liselle offered her the horsehair chair.

"Liselle, I don't know what to say—what to think—you're a Wintersted?!"

"I never intended to hide it, Lucy, I'm sorry I surprised you like I did."

"Why didn't you tell me?"

Liselle reached for her hand. "My name never came up; then when we found the cottage it seemed awkward to explain. Not to mention my surprise. I didn't know my father lived here; I was three when he died. When you told me his story, I was shocked." Liselle paused to take a deep breath, "Along the way, we became friends. I'm sorry if I hurt you."

"My grandmother cared deeply for the Wintersteds," Lucy explained, "I guess everyone lost track after the drowning. I certainly didn't know Hank had a second family, but I do welcome the cottage being inhabited again and, by some great stroke of fate, with a Wintersted."

Liselle hugged her. "Thank you Lucy, you don't know how much that means to me."

"You just should have told me," Lucy admonished.

"I'm truly sorry that I didn't find a way sooner," Liselle apologized. "But, I do have a great idea! Why don't you stay here tonight?"

Lucy looked at her dumbfounded. "Me stay here? Oh, hardly—where would I sleep?"

"You can see how comfortable it is and tomorrow we can walk to church."

"Where would I sleep, Liselle, where would I sleep?"

"I have cushions, pillows, sleeping bag. I can make you a bed. And I can whip up a mean little omelet on the stove. Come on Lucy, give it a try! Let me repay you for all you've done!"

"Well, maybe," Lucy relented, not at all sure. "I'll have to run home for a few things and tell Emily not to fix supper."

"Great! Whenever you're ready, come over, I'm going to tidy up a little."

7

AFTER LUCY LEFT, LISELLE discovered the photo album from Captain's trunk among her books. She remembered pushing it under Grandmother's bed the night before; in the morning Lucy must have thought it was hers and put it with her things.

Taking a deep breath, she ventured another look. There were pictures of Grandmother and Lucy's parents, and Lucy at different ages. At the back was a photo of Hank and Lizzie in wedding attire and photos of adorable twin boys sitting on their laps. Lizelle had never seen a picture of her father as a young man. He looked happy.

She knew that Lizzie had died a few years before Hank met and married her mother; yet it felt odd to see him with another woman. George was already grown when her parents married and bitterly opposed to his father replacing his mother. He never visited Hank after that.

All these things Liselle had learned from Mother but she had never heard about the Wintersted tragedy. Now she wondered if Mother knew. Surely she wouldn't have kept this information from her.

It occurred to her that the twin who died was her half-brother and suddenly she felt compelled to honor his memory, perhaps soothe the ache of his loss and rummaging through her art supplies, she selected paints and brushes before walking to the shed.

Slinging the satchel over her shoulder, she climbed down the slippery bank to balance on the rocks. Stretching as high as possible, she could just reach the top of the stilt and began to paint it light blue. When she reached the water's edge, she climbed back up the bank and where the stilt joined the shed, she painted a wreath of green leaves and pink flowers. Across the top she lettered 'safe in the arms of Jesus' and in the center 'Grant Wintersted'.

Standing back to appraise her work, on impulse she ran to the house and returned with a staple gun and handful of rainbow-colored ribbons.

Attached to the lower edge of the wreath, they fluttered in the breeze and wrapped around the newly painted stilt. Now the place where Grant died so many years ago had been memorialized, time and distance making it possible for her to do what his parents were unable to do: honor the place where he lived and died.

Cleaning her brushes in the kitchen sink, she realized another thread connected her to Hank: that of deep loss and wondered why George claimed to be working for his father. Hank had been dead for 23 years. Did her father leave some provision for the cottage or was George merely preserving the memory of a dead brother for a family that never recovered from its loss?

She heard a car door slam and Lucy stuck her head in the front door. "Liselle?"

"Here in the kitchen!"

"What have you been doing?"

"Oh, fixing a few things, go look at the shed."

Lucy set her things on the kitchen table and walked out the side door. "What a nice thing to do!" she offered. "So his name was Grant."

"Yes, it needed something, you know; so bleak and gray, the tragedy of it and all." They watched the ribbons lifting on the breeze.

"Well, I think it's perfect," responded Lucy. "I'm still surprised about you being a Wintersted. I don't know if I would have run on like I did about Hank and Lizzie."

"You only told the truth, Lucy, and it was such a long time ago."

After a supper of sandwiches and soup Liselle stoked the fire in the Franklin and they relaxed with steaming mugs of cider as Lucy described different families on the island. Later Liselle arranged Lucy's sleeping bag in the back bedroom before she settled on quilts in the front bedroom.

They slept soundly that night, not even the gusts of wind rattling the windows disturbed them. Perhaps that's why they didn't hear someone creep across the porch or the whoosh of an aerosol can.

~

When Liselle got up the next morning she was shocked to see the cryptic message sprayed across the glass, "leave or be burned out". She waited until Lucy woke to break the news. Lucy was deeply troubled. Who cared about the Wintersted place?

"You should file a police report," Lucy insisted.

"No police," Liselle decided. "This is probably someone surprised to see the place occupied or kids just messing around."

Right now she was more concerned about who owned the cottage and her father's intentions. Perhaps it was time to visit Olympia and explore mother's safe deposit box, contact her father's attorney.

"I plan to take the bus to Olympia and visit my father's attorney, Lucy. You're welcome to come."

"When do you go?"

"Tomorrow, I want to attend church with you today."

"I'll drive you to Olympia, you needn't worry about that," Lucy offered.

"Thank you, Lucy."

"Good," Lucy replied, "After church let's get your things and go to my place. Emily can get our breakfast in the morning and we can get an early start."

On the walk to church, Lucy struggled to breathe and they rested on a shady bench as a blue jay screeched overhead. When the church bells began to chime, Lucy led the way through arched doors into the sanctuary where antique glass windows cast a warm glow over the gently worn benches. It was a welcoming place and Liselle breathed deeply of the peaceful surroundings, basking in the thought that her Grandmother had cared for the community's spiritual needs.

They entered the McGivens' pew and were about to sit when a tall robust lady swooped over to hug Lucy. Swaddled in cream wool with gold chains flopping over her ample bosom, "Lucy Vankosky, where have you been all week?" she shrilled in a highly-cultured voice. "You missed guild!"

Lucy was not pleased to see her. As the lady turned to study Liselle, Lucy hurriedly introduced them. "Frieda Vankosky Harmeyer, this is Liselle Wintersted," she said.

Liselle saw the surprised look on Frieda's face, but before she could respond the pastor announced the first song and Frieda retreated to her pew two rows back. Lucy smiled as they opened their hymn books.

At the end of service, Frieda was surrounded by friends and couldn't get back to them. "It's a blessing," Lucy whispered, "She's a nosy gossip."

At the cottage Liselle threw a few things into a bag, scraped paint off the window and Lucy drove them to the mansion. "A penny for your thoughts . . ." Lucy said.

"Oh, I don't know if they're worth that much! I'm trying to decide how long this trip will take. I don't want to leave right now, but I must so I can clear up things."

"What sort of things?"

"When we return, I think it will make more sense, that is, if I can find my father's attorney and he can answer my questions. Then I will tell you everything, I promise."

Lucy went in her den to leave instructions for the staff while Liselle went to Grandmother's room. Dumping her things on the rug near Captain's trunk, she noticed the crystal vase was empty. "Nyls must be running late today," she thought as she settled on the bed with a journal. She heard the doorbell ring as she dozed off.

July 28, 1929

Wilson brought Lizzie with him when he delivered the eggs. I loaned her more books and will inquire about her help with Franklin a few afternoons a week.

EM

≈

Lucy in robe and slippers had just settled in her den when Frieda barged in, gold chains bouncing and talking before her coat was off. "Listen, Lucy, we've known each other a long time and I've never heard of any Liselle Wintersted. Who is she and what is Emily saying about you going to Olympia tomorrow? What is going on?" Frieda demanded.

Irritated by the interruption, Lucy didn't especially feel like explaining herself. "Frieda, is this your idea of friendship? To barge in and expect me to stop what I'm doing to be interrogated by you?"

Caught short and considered a lady of proper breeding, Frieda was unbalanced by Lucy's accusation for Lucy was normally a pushover before her steamroller ways. "Uh, no," Frieda began. "Are you going to offer me tea?" she finished lamely.

"I think we can arrange that." Lucy rang for Emily and they settled in chairs away from her writing desk as Frieda twisted her rings and waited for Emily to serve them.

"Lucy," Frieda began again, "I would like to hear about your week, and why you feel it necessary to take off for Olympia? From what I've heard, you just met this Liselle and nowadays you have to be careful. And what about your asthma and getting it all stirred up?"

"Frieda, I have never felt better! As for having just met Liselle, I feel that I do know her. There is something very comforting about her. And despite our obvious age difference, we have become friends."

Frieda struggled to understand as Lucy continued, "It doesn't matter what you say. At this point I've made up my mind, I'm going and I intend to have a wonderful time."

They finished their tea in silence as Frieda sent dubious glances at her old friend, obviously divided over this newcomer. Lucy's actions made no sense to her.

After Frieda left, in a much quieter tone than she arrived, Lucy slipped down the hall to Liselle's room and pushed on the slightly open door. Her eyes widened as they adjusted in the dim light to the message on the bureau mirror: "do not ignore me".

"Oh, no," Lucy dashed to the bathroom as Liselle woke. Returning with a damp towel she began dabbing at the mirror.

"What's wrong?" Liselle rubbed her eyes.

"You won't believe, in my own house. I can't believe it! I can't believe anyone would come in here with you sleeping here . . . now don't you worry, we'll figure this out," Lucy soothed, patting Liselle's hand. "I came to tell you that dinner's ready."

"Thanks, but I don't think I could eat right now," Liselle admitted.

As Lucy left, Liselle dropped to her knees and picked up her Bible, her stomach twisting in knots. Psalm 138 fell open before her: "*Though I walk in the midst of trouble, you preserve my life; you stretch out your hand against the anger of my foes, with your right hand you save me.*"

She admitted she was frightened: too many mysteries, too many losses; now this unexpected chipping away at her newfound security; threats from some unknown source–twice in one weekend. Was she upsetting someone by stirring up the past?

"Lord Jesus, I need your peace." She felt his strength and wanted to remain longer in his presence. Reluctantly she breathed a quick thank you to her best friend and left to join Lucy. As she did, she noticed that fresh flowers now filled the vase.

8

EARLY THE NEXT MORNING, driving east toward the interstate, Lucy recited more area history. "This is Old Byrd Mill road, a major route between Steilacoom and the Puyallup Valley and heavily used by farmers and lumberjacks." As if to prove her point, pickups and log trucks clogged their way.

Merging onto Interstate 5 in the steady flow of traffic going south, the speeding pavement seemed to mesmerize Liselle and she enjoyed the quiet until Lucy broke the spell.

"I know it's personal, Liselle, but I was curious how you reacted to that horrible message yesterday. Do you always pray?"

"I guess I do; actually prayer is just talking to God."

"I've heard the pastor say that," Lucy replied, "but it seems like the sort of churchy thing he's supposed to say. To me, God seems far away!"

"I've felt that way Lucy, but God is about a relationship, like the song we sang yesterday 'What a Friend we have in Jesus'."

"But God already knows my needs."

"Yes, but He loves your uniqueness and wants a discourse with you. His son is the very presence of God in our lives."

Lucy was silent as she reflected on her words. "Since Leonard passed away I haven't had the same enthusiasm for life. Len had a unique approach to God and I drew on that for strength, he helped me believe. With him gone, I feel deserted by both."

"Well, I can certainly identify with the desertion part."

"You can?"

"Yes, my dad Hank, you know, died before I ever got to know him, and sometimes my view of God as a father was fuzzy because I didn't have a dad. I went through a period where I was mad at God, didn't understand His ways, didn't feel like He was close at all. Then one day my mom said, 'If you don't feel close to God, guess who moved?' She helped me understand that God promised to never leave me. And she helped me appreciate all the things that God has given us."

"I never really thought about everything coming from God. Obviously I've taken a lot for granted," Lucy confessed. "And I can tell that your mother was a great influence. I know I would have loved her, too."

"When Mother got sick last year, I prayed my brains out, convinced that her survival was crucial to my survival. Then the worst happened and I had no choice but to go through it, and in the process I learned that God was right there beside me, opening doors I couldn't see and teaching me lessons I wouldn't learn. But the greatest event since then has been meeting you, Lucy, and God orchestrated that. There's no other way to explain it."

Lucy blushed at the compliment. A few minutes later she spotted their exit and took the off ramp to Ellen's house. Liselle wasn't ready to put her memories in storage just yet and had yet to decide what to do with her mother's things. With the mortgage paid off, she didn't know if she would return to Olympia. For the time she would keep the house how mother left it.

As Lucy turned into the driveway, Liselle pulled the garage door opener from her backpack and didn't notice Jackson's letter fall to the floor.

Instructing Lucy to park in the garage and loaded with bags they walked through a breezeway to enter the kitchen, Liselle leading the way to the living room.

"Get comfortable and we'll put our things away later," she directed as she fluffed cushions and opened drapes. "I'll fix lunch while you relax."

Lucy sank on the sofa to study the cozy sitting room. She and Len had spent a fortune furnishing a house bigger than anything they would ever need, yet this tiny room with its elegant decor was just as beautiful.

A couch in pale yellow with pops of teal and melon rugs and pillows; drapes in soft sage and light that filtered through the plantation blinds. It was obvious Ellen had had extraordinary good taste and loved beautiful things as reflected in the antique tables and carefully selected art.

Liselle returned with a lunch tray and placed it on the coffee table. "Lucy, how well did you know George Wintersted," she asked.

"Not very," Lucy responded. "I hadn't seen him in years! Didn't even know it was him that was working on the cottage. He rarely visited the island and I didn't pay much attention to the place. The tragedy happened before I was born. Why do you ask?"

"I was wondering if you thought he had something to do with spray painting the window Saturday night. That doesn't explain the mirror at your house but I just wondered what you thought of him?"

"I guess if George vandalized the house, why would he rent it in the first place, especially after fixing it up?"

"Good point, Lucy." They moved to the kitchen to clean up, Liselle feeling restless after the long car ride. "What do you say we go sightseeing? Olympia is a beautiful city with turn of the century buildings and the capitol grounds are quite gorgeous this time of year," she suggested. "I can be your guide!"

∾

Lucy drove to the capitol and they toured the Rotunda with its Alaskan gray marble and five ton Tiffany chandeliers, then strolled around Sylvester Park touring the Veteran Memorials and Governor's mansion before going to the Farmers' Market.

At Percival Landing they discovered a seafood restaurant. As the setting sun was mirrored in the sparkling waves, they were seated at a window booth and sipped tea while their entrees were prepared.

"Tell me about Frieda, you've been friends a long time."

"Oh, forever," Lucy exclaimed. "It began with Grandmother. She and Frieda's grandmother, Willadean Vankosky loved to shop. Mrs. Vankosky had two sons–one lost at sea, the other Frieda's father. Frieda and I played together and remained close over the years. Now with Len gone she likes to think she's my guardian!"

"It must be nice to have a friend that close and caring," Liselle added.

"Yes and no," Lucy continued. "Even though Frieda lives on the other side of the island, we have such large estates that her property actually backs up to mine. She keeps an eye on everything I do."

"That must feel odd?"

"Actually *strangled* is more like it! You remember the little duck pond behind the house?"

"Yes, I thought it a nice touch," replied Liselle.

"Well, Frieda didn't want it there. I had it put in a few years ago and Frieda didn't like the idea of animals on the place. She prefers sea gulls flying along the shore, not sitting ducks!"

Liselle burst out laughing but Lucy smiled and continued. "Oh, there's more! Frieda's brother was Leonard Vankosky. But he was so different from her, always gentle, kind and pleasant. That's what attracted me to him . . ."

"Why you're Frieda's sister-in-law!"

"Yes! And since I have no heirs, I am the last of the McGivens, Frieda's children will inherit everything. Even if I didn't leave my estate to her because of our long friendship, she is Len's sister and my only family." They were silent before Lucy added, "I would have preferred the house go to a McGivens, but that won't ever happen."

Liselle's mind was racing again. How long before she felt comfortable enough to explain her search for her grandmother? And Lucy's latest revelation seemed to justify Frieda's unfriendly attitude. As they left the restaurant Liselle prayed, "Lord, show me how to do this."

They returned to the bungalow and retired to their bedrooms, Liselle finding it easier to be in her mother's house after being away the last few months. Living on the island had helped in the healing process for on Anderson she had no history with Ellen. As her life adapted to a new pace, she no longer felt constant grief and owed that sense of peace to Lucy and to God.

Wait on the Lord; once again good advice from her mother.

9

THE NEXT MORNING LISELLE borrowed Lucy's van and arrived at the bank as it was opening. After the clerk checked her documents, they entered the vault, located the box, and the clerk positioned her key in sequence with Liselle's. The deposit drawer slid open and the clerk left her to sort through the papers.

At the very bottom was a letter addressed to her father from the law firm of Synder, Evans & Wells, signed by Joseph Scudder, her father's attorney. Promptly she telephoned the firm and scheduled a meeting with Mr. Scudder for that afternoon. Leaving her telephone number with the receptionist and with a couple of hours to spare, she drove home to review the rest of the documents. When she arrived, Lucy met her at the door.

"Your father's attorney called, a Mr. Scudder. He sounded very anxious to meet you, wants you to join him for lunch at the Little Italy."

"That sounds great, why don't you join us?"

"Well," Lucy hesitated. "If you think it will be all right?"

"Yes, absolutely, I don't think there will be any huge surprises and I want you there."

At the Little Italy the waitress led them to a table in a private room in back. As they approached, a stately gentleman rose to greet them.

"Miss Wintersted?" he inquired.

"Yes," Liselle offered her hand, "Mr. Scudder, so nice to meet you!"

"My pleasure," he said, bowing slightly. She noticed his warm blue eyes and silver hair that skimmed his collar and flowed away from a deeply tanned face.

"This is my friend, Lucy Vankosky."

"A pleasure, Ms. Vankosky, please be seated, ladies." He pulled out chairs for them and turning to Liselle, he added, "I was sorry to learn of your mother's passing."

"Thank you, Mr. Scudder. It has been difficult without her."

"I can imagine. I didn't know her as well as your father, she took her legal matters elsewhere, but I know she was a great comfort to your father, who was a dear friend of mine. I am happy to finally meet you."

"Thank you for your kind words."

"What can I do for you today, Miss Wintersted?"

"Please, call me Liselle. First of all, I relocated to Anderson Island last week." She paused as she noticed the change in his expression, his eyes narrowing slightly, perhaps only to listen more closely, before she continued, "Quite by accident–except I don't believe it was an accident–I found and rented a house on the island, a small cottage actually, that my father built."

"How interesting," Mr. Scudder interjected, "and who rented this house to you?"

"George Wintersted; he was repairing it. My question—my concern is—to whom does the house belong? Did my father keep it for a special reason; did it go to George?"

The old lawyer looked Liselle directly in the eye and confidently she returned his gaze, trusting him, liking him. "Liselle Wintersted, I have a letter for you from your father. I have kept it since before his death with instructions to give it to you if you ever came seeking answers. Your father wanted you to know the history of the Wintersteds, but only if you asked."

Inwardly she felt herself recoil. The attorney knew about her, was perhaps expecting her? With trembling hand she took the bulky envelope as Lucy squeezed her knee. "But what if I had never asked?"

"Your father didn't want to impose this on you if you didn't want to be bothered," he replied. "It's that simple. Your father was not a complicated man. His life may have been, but he tried to keep his part in it simple. He wanted you to know only what you wanted to know, he wasn't especially interested in history or the keeping of it. Perhaps that was due to the losses he suffered. However, your father and I go back a long way and I have to say that's how our generation approached the unpredictable parts of life."

He paused to sip his coffee before continuing, "We survived a world war and the Great Depression, not to mention burying wives and children along the way, so our viewpoints were similar. Whatever you may think about the arrangements your father made, I tend to agree with him. I can certainly understand his reasoning."

Liselle sensed the lawyer defending his old friend. At her silence, Mr. Scudder suggested she wait until she was home to read the letter. "For now let's enjoy lunch. I have waited a long time to meet Hank's only daughter and lunch is my treat. If you have more questions I will be happy to meet with you again."

"Yes, thank you, I like that idea," said Liselle stuffing the letter in her bag and turning her attention to the menu. She liked Joseph Scudder, so kind and gracious; she was pleased to think that her father had been like him in his views, perhaps even in his distinguished appearance.

They enjoyed a lively lunch as Mr. Scudder and Lucy tried to outdo each other with fishing stories off the San Juan Islands, both agreeing that Anacortes and Orcas Island were excellent spots.

After saying good-bye, Liselle and Lucy spent the remainder of the afternoon beach combing. The day was unusually warm and the always proper Lucy surprised herself by removing her shoes to wade in the surf. The setting sun finally drove them back to shore.

The evening had turned chilly and they retired early, Liselle pleased that the meeting with the attorney had gone so well. She pulled her father's letter from her handbag and studied the handwriting. For the past twenty plus years it had lain in the attorney's confidential files, but the writing was still legible. Taking a deep breath, she broke the seal and began to read:

> My little Liselle,
> January 20, 1973
>
> Today you are three! How fast time goes. It seems only yesterday I first held you, my treasure in old age. I don't know how long I will be here, but I do know that if some day you read this, it will be because you have grown into an intelligent, mature woman, ready to face the challenges of life and seeking answers. Hence I have given this to my dear friend Joseph for safekeeping. I know your mother will understand when the time comes.
>
> If you have gotten so far as to find Joseph and have this letter, then you have probably learned something of my life before I met your mother. You possibly know that George had a twin brother, Grant, who drowned. Perhaps you have even discovered the little house I built.
>
> I built it for the first woman I loved, Lizzie, and determined that next in line it should belong to you. Every nail, every board, was put together with love. This succession is not intended to by-pass my Ellen, but merely to assure the transfer to you.
>
> [Upon my death, the details of the inheritance will be sealed and George instructed to maintain it. For that he will be

compensated, for I know he has no interest in ever living there because of his brother.]

Should you never claim the house, it will pass to the historical society. Should you claim it, maintenance payments to George will cease 30 days after you give notice of intent to exercise your right to inherit.

Knowing your mother's zeal for our faith, I know she will raise you in God's truth. With such hope I can say that we will be together again someday at the throne of Jesus, there to thank Him for His great gift of salvation.

Remember that what seems like a lifetime on earth is less than a millisecond in heaven; so make it count, my daughter and God bless you Liz-El. Until then, all my love,

Father

She wept then; the part about mother and father's assumption, along with hers, that mom would always be there; the realization that the little house was hers. She loved the little house, the fact that she had only to claim it was more then she had hoped.

She felt a pang of disappointment that George had let it fall into disrepair. Well, that was about to change. For the first time, she understood how her name had been crafted. Father had chosen it to honor his two wives.

Putting the letter aside, she turned off the lamp and cried great sobs into her pillow, mourning the loss of her parents. Finally she slept, damp hair pulled across one shoulder, tossing and turning with dreadful dreams.

Father in the garden while mother watered flowers; beyond them a lady with long red hair fed ducks; as Liselle ran toward her, she kept moving away and unable to reach her, Liselle turned back alone by her parents' graves.

Bright sunlight streaming in the window woke her and a dull headache throbbed across the top of her head. Pulling on a robe she stumbled to the kitchen where Lucy whistled a tune as coffee brewed and pancakes steamed on the griddle. One glance at Liselle and she moved to pour coffee and place it before her on the table. "You didn't sleep well?"

"No, I had a bad dream, a sad dream, I'm not sure coffee will help."

"I'm sorry; tell me about it?" Lucy sat down opposite her.

"The letter from my father . . . was upsetting." She paused as Lucy waited expectantly. "My father preserved the house for me," she blurted as fresh tears fell.

"Oh, honey, there now, that's grand isn't it?" Lucy struggled to hold back her own tears.

"Ye-e-s," Liselle sobbed. "It was just the whole tone of the letter, the fresh reminder that my parents are gone, never getting to know my father; losing my mother!"

By now Lucy was crying, too, fat tears rolling down her cheeks. "There, there, it's okay to cry. I know how you feel, I know how you feel."

Liselle struggled to regain her composure. "You can read the letter if you want, but one thing is certain—I want to exercise my right to inherit and give George his thirty days' notice. Do you know how to contact him?"

The question helped Lucy focus. "Let's see, last I heard he lived in Kent. Anyway, it's such a small city I can't imagine a letter wouldn't find him. Or better yet, Mr. Scudder knows the details; it's his job to handle this. Why don't you call him and let him know your intentions?"

"Lucy, what would I do without you?"

"Well," she said modestly, "I'm sure he's expecting to hear from you. Now, how about some pancakes?"

After breakfast Liselle called Mr. Scudder to start the transfer of the deed to the cottage. That done, she still puzzled over why Grandmother had given away her baby girl. Where was her family?

As they washed dishes, she asked "Lucy, what do you know about your grandmother before she moved to the island? I mean, did she have any relatives?"

"Gosh, I don't know," Lucy replied, "I never really thought about it. I guess I was used to being an only child, same as my father. I probably thought Grandmother didn't have any siblings either. Except for that strong sense of someone missing in her life, I didn't think about it much. But it was around Christmas every year, and then into the spring that Grandmother would get pensive . . . melancholy. As I got older I began to pick up on those nuances."

Lucy paused, "Now that you mention it, it seems odd that Grandmother didn't mention relatives. I don't recall seeing pictures of other family members. My mother wasn't from the island and didn't pay much attention to the McGivens' history. Still, how odd that the subject never came up!"

They were silent before Lucy continued, "You know, there must be school records in Steilacoom, that's where my grandparents met. Maybe that's why I always had the feeling that Grandmother was missing somebody–who knows, maybe there is family around!"

Her mind was in high gear, working on the riddle. "Why don't we go back to Anderson today?"

Gathering their things, Liselle called Mr. Scudder's secretary to leave Lucy's phone number. With van loaded, they headed north as Lucy outlined her plan to visit the library, schools, and town hall for records. She would track down any information if it existed.

"I know Grandmother's family name was Cottington—Elizabeth Cottington," Lucy explained.

They reached Steilacoom just in time for the ferry. As Lucy dropped Liselle at the cottage she asked, "How are you getting to work in the morning?"

"I'll just jog to the ferry. I'm used to it!"

"Well, I'm catching the ferry early to start the hunt. Why don't you grab a ride with me and I'll pick you up after your shift."

"Okay, then you can fill me in on what you find!"

"Sure, plan to come for dinner."

10

God sets the lonely in families;
he leads forth the desolate in a homeland.

PSALM 68:5

THE NEXT DAY LISELLE hoped Lucy was having more success in her search than she was at work, mixing up several customers' orders. Jana was sympathetic when she explained that she had spent her time moving to Anderson Island and taking care of legal matters in Olympia.

Over the course of working at the restaurant Liselle had shared her heartache over her mother's death and was able to get time off as needed, but she certainly didn't want to abuse her employer's kindness.

Four o'clock came and Liselle finished serving her last table; then dashed for the back to change into sweats. Lucy waited at the curb with a big grin on her face.

"What did you find out?" Liselle asked as she hopped in the van.

"You won't believe it!" Lucy exclaimed. "Grandmother went through all twelve grades *in* the Steilacoom district."

"No!"

"Yes, but she didn't graduate. I found that really odd, maybe she got sick or something, to go through almost twelve grades, so I checked old papers, small town papers are quite chatty, but I didn't find any mention of an accident or illness. Only that her name was not listed among the graduating seniors. Then I checked the hospital ledger and payday, an Elizabeth Cottington was listed as a patient in March of 1926! She would have been about seventeen."

Liselle felt a shiver go up her spine; her mother was born March 20th of that year. "So, were you able to find out why she was admitted?"

"No, the trail stops there–cold," Lucy said.

"Do you remember the dates of her admission?" Liselle asked.

"Around the 20th maybe . . ." Lucy explained. Liselle didn't say anything as Lucy pulled into her driveway. She was tired and hungry, didn't want to think anymore.

~

After dinner Liselle had a proposal. "Lucy, are you up to going through that old trunk again?" she asked.

"What do you mean?"

"Well, we didn't open the ebony box last time–maybe now is a good time? Maybe it has some personal effect of Grandmother's, maybe a clue?"

Lucy jumped on the word *clue*. "Yeah, how about something important being there all these years right under our noses and nobody ever saw it!"

They hurried to Grandmother's room and flung open the trunk, expecting to find the ebony box on top. After a careful search it was located near the bottom.

"I was beginning to think we had lost it!" Lucy exclaimed and sitting down on the rug beside Liselle, she asked, "Are you ready?"

"Let's do it!"

Running her finger over the polished top and her grandmother's initials, Lucy pulled the tiny clasp and popped the lid. Inside a single sheet of paper lay neatly folded. Disappointment flooded Lucy's face. "Just a piece of paper," she exclaimed setting the box down.

"Let's read it." Liselle took the paper from her hand, recognizing Grandmother's familiar script and she began to read out loud:

> *To the finder of this locket, let the hunter take care,*
> *A heart broken in two needs love to repair.*
> *May the holder of the other half find this true.*
> *What was torn apart by circumstance may someday be made new.*

"What do you make of it," Lucy asked and looked in the box again. There on the velvet lining, previously hidden, was half a silver heart.

"What do you suppose it means?" Lucy puzzled out loud. "And the heart looks familiar, like I've seen it before. Oh-h-h, this is nerve-wracking!"

Liselle felt light headed, thinking about the pendant concealed beneath her sweater. "Lucy, I thought you liked mysteries!"

"I do, but I like them best when they're solved. That's the whole point! I can't stand so many unanswered questions. I'm going to bed, why don't you stay here tonight. Grandmother's room is always ready for you."

"Thanks, Lucy I do have an early shift."

Liselle crawled into the four-poster with Grandmother's journal and noted the date was over three years after the hospital stay.

November 22, 1929

I thought I lost my heart pendant today when Franklin tugged on the chain and it flew across the room. I found it after several frantic minutes of searching. Now safe in the ebony box Captain brought on his last trip, I won't risk losing it again—this sweet reminder of my "other life".

EM

∼

Liselle woke the next morning thinking about Grandmother's journal entry. It felt like she was reaching across time with the poem, journal, and an insignificant piece of jewelry. On a hunch, Liselle slipped the heart from her neck, removed the other half from the box and with quivering fingers placed them together. A perfect fit. For the first time she noticed that the rounded E on her pendant was facing backwards; when placed together the two Es formed a circle in the center of a completed heart.

Elizabeth and Ellen: again she was struck by the unfairness of her mother never knowing about her birth mother or half brother, Lucy's father, her niece Lucinda. How wrong, how selfish of her grandparents to keep this from them!

"*Forgive them,*" she heard the still small Voice remind.

"Yes, Lord," she breathed, "Forgiveness is a choice, help me. I don't want to be angry. I know they loved us."

She picked up the journal and read again last night's passage. What was that "other life" that Grandmother referred to and did it do any good to pursue this—or was it better to leave the past alone? Did Grandmother leave clues, hoping to right some wrong? Was it time to tell Lucy?

If she waited too long, Lucy might stumble on the truth and suspect her of having wrong motives for withholding this information. She didn't want a repeat of the misunderstanding over her name.

Bounding off the bed, she raced across the room to telephone the restaurant. "Jana, I really need to take today off, is it okay?"

"I think you can take a break," Jana replied. "And it's been slow this week, don't worry about us."

"Thanks Jana, you're a peach," she said.

Pulling on jeans and oversized shirt, Liselle brushed her hair straight back, tied it with a ribbon and added pearl earrings. The heart necklace that she always wore hugged her neck and dipped beneath her shirt as she paused to study her figure in the bathroom mirror. Friends had teased her during the teen years for being a string-bean, now she was lithe while they battled extra pounds.

Her eyes glowed with excitement and her heart pounded with hope. She felt good, she felt happy! And she loved Lucy, her cousin!

In the kitchen, Lucy squealed with pleasure when Liselle explained her plan. "I promise I will explain everything after breakfast," she assured.

Having collected several items and placed them in her back pack, Liselle walked with Lucy to the duck pond, the sun warm and welcoming, Lucy wearing a wide-brimmed hat while Liselle turned her face to the sun.

Settling on the autumn-dried grass, a few ducks approached and Liselle tossed bread crusts their way. Fall was her favorite time of year with its breathtaking beauty and clear sweet air. Still, she felt apprehensive and took a deep breath to calm herself.

Seven months had passed since Ellen's death; yet on this day the thought came with a sense of peace, the hurt beginning to heal into hope. She could go on, something she had not thought possible on the day of the funeral and owed this newfound strength to Lucy.

Balanced on her hands and knees with backpack beside her, she leaned towards Lucy and began, "You remember I told you that my mother died earlier this year?"

"Yes," agreed Lucy.

"What I didn't tell you was that immediately after the funeral my grandparents told me they were not her biological parents!"

"For real," Lucy exclaimed!

"For real, they adopted my mother in Steilacoom and never told anyone. At the time they received two personal items with the baby, a photo and . . ."

"And w*hat*," Lucy questioned; a puzzled look on her face.

Liselle fingered the small heart that had slipped from beneath her shirt.

"Why are you wearing Grandmother's necklace," Lucy queried.

Liselle tucked the heart protectively inside her shirt. "It's not . . . Grandmother's," she explained. "This necklace came with my mother when she was adopted by my grandparents."

Lucy hesitated. "With your mother . . . ?"

"Yes, my mother was born in Steilacoom on March 20, 1926, the same date your grandmother was hospitalized."

"So . . ." Lucy began.

"And the birth mother's photograph that my grandparents received is identical to the one of Elizabeth in her photo album!" Liselle laid the two photos side by side: "This from your grandmother's album and this from my grandparents."

Lucy studied the photos as Liselle opened Grandmother's journal. "And look at this entry by Grandmother dated November 22, 1929: *this necklace is a sweet reminder of my "other life"*. She wrote that over three years after her hospitalization. And the poem, Lucy, read it again:

> *To the finder of this locket, let the hunter take care,*
> *A heart broken in two needs love to repair.*
> *May the holder of the other half find this true,*
> *What was torn apart by circumstance may someday be made new.*

You read mysteries, Lucy, don't you see a pattern?"

Liselle waited for her response.

"This is weird," Lucy admitted. "I mean I read about things like this in novels, but not in real life."

"I think fiction mimics life, Lucy. To me, life is a colossal mystery, maybe not always as intense as a grandmother having a past, or a father hiding a little cottage for a daughter who *might* or *might not someday discover* it. The unexpected happens to ordinary people all the time!"

"How long have you known, Liselle?" Lucy asked in a whisper.

"I don't know how long for sure, Lucy. I came to Steilacoom hoping to find information about my mother's family. With only sketchy details, it was a long shot to think I might actually find anyone. The Wintersted cottage was a total surprise. Look at the photos—this from my grandparents—this from Grandmother's album."

Liselle paused as Lucy's silence stretched out. "And look how the necklace fits together, both halves perfectly," Liselle continued, removing her necklace and placing the two together.

"Liselle," Lucy said slowly, "Does—this—mean—we—are *cousins*?"

"Well, it sure looks like it to me and I like it! I realize I've had longer to get used to the idea, but . . ." Her words were cut short as Lucy struggled to her feet, grabbed Liselle's shoulders and began dancing around her. "*Family*–I have *family*!" she shouted.

Liselle jumped to her feet and joined the dance. "We're family," she screamed as the ducks squawked loudly and fled to the other side of the pond.

Laughing, Liselle shouted, "Lucy, what will Frieda think?"

"Oh, I hope she sees us out here acting like we've lost our minds," Lucy gasped. "It will give her something to talk about!"

Out of breath, they fell in a heap on the grass, wiping tears from their eyes.

"One thing I'd like, Liselle, if you don't mind?"

"Sure . . . ?"

"You wear your mother's necklace and I'll wear Grandmother's and together we'll make a whole like she wanted."

"It's a deal!"

As they walked back to the house, Cecelia met them at the kitchen door.

"Miss Liselle, you had a message from a law firm in Olympia. I didn't know where you were so I wrote it down."

"Thank you, Cecelia."

Her eyes widened as she read:

Mr. Scudder died in his sleep last night. Your matter has been reassigned to Tom Caribou of our firm. He will call you next week.

1 1

AFTER LISELLE GOT OFF the phone, she found Lucy in her study. "It's going to be a small, private funeral in Olympia."

"How's his secretary holding up?" asked Lucy.

"Peggy is doing pretty well, I guess, she was with him a long time and it was just so unexpected."

"What about this Tom Caribou, who is he?" Lucy continued.

"Well, according to Peggy, he's a young lawyer, out of law school a couple of years. I certainly don't need any powerhouse attorney for my legal work. It's all pretty straightforward just claiming what's legally mine. Of course I don't want to be put on a shelf and forgotten so I asked Peggy why I wouldn't hear from him for a week."

"What'd she say?" inquired Lucy.

"He's fishing in Alaska! Oh, and the good news is that Mr. Scudder had started the paperwork. The new attorney just needs to verify the deed, property taxes and boundary lines, things like that."

～

Having freely discussed their new-found kinship, word traveled swiftly around the island. When they told the household staff, Emily was delighted; Cecelia smiled her shy smile, and Nyls mumbled congratulations before shuffling off to mulch flowerbeds. Liselle wondered again at his silence but didn't have long to ponder with the arrival of Frieda for what Lucy referred to as her "weekly check-up". As Liselle sat in the kitchen with Emily, she heard Frieda go into Lucy's study.

"Emily, I'll just go in the music room and practice the piano," Liselle explained.

It seemed best for her to stay out of sight for she sensed Frieda's dislike and didn't want a confrontation. Besides, she could use the practice. Debussy's *Clair de Lune* with its crossover scales and minor notes was proving a challenge to master.

Sitting on the piano stool with hands arched to begin, a memory of mother came, of playing *Heart and Soul* together, one of the first pieces Ellen had taught her. "Lord, let me take such delight in children some day," she prayed.

~

"Lucy this is absolutely preposterous! I've never heard of such a thing," Frieda stormed around the room. "The girl's a gold-digger, that's all, knows how to tell a convincing story! It's obvious she has her sights set on your place!"

Lucy held up her hand. "Peace, Frieda, you really need to calm down! It's all perfectly legitimate. The proof is there, I'm satisfied with it and I might add, happy, to have found a blood relative. I'm sorry if this messes up your plans."

"Whatever are you talking about?" Frieda demanded.

"Well, obviously you had hoped to join our estates so your children would have a larger inheritance."

"That's an insult, Lucy, to accuse me of only caring about your property!"

"Then what exactly is your concern, Frieda?" Lucy asked. Frieda stood blinking, her concentration broken as Lucy continued, "I know for a fact, Frieda, that Liselle has no interest in this place, except possibly because it belonged to our grandmother. I think her right to inherit is considerable."

"Well consider this," Frieda blustered. "She has no right–her mother was adopted into another family! Why, the very idea!"

"Oh, but I can acknowledge her as Grandmother's long lost heir," Lucy shot back. "There's not a court in the land that would deny me that, especially if Grandmother, as a minor, was forced to give up her baby."

Lucy found herself making a strong defense, her upbringing having instilled in her a strong sense of right and wrong and the ability, when necessary, to defend those values.

"Frieda, I really think you should leave and come back when you're in a more pleasant mood," she suggested.

"I can assure you I'm not going to be in a more *pleasant* mood over this," Frieda threatened as she picked up her coat and stormed out.

Liselle entered the study when she heard the front door slam. "I'm sorry this is causing trouble."

"Oh, nonsense," Lucy exclaimed, "it's time Frieda learns that everything doesn't always go her way! I'm going to do what I think Grandmother would have wanted. Think how differently things would have turned out if she hadn't lost your mother," Lucy explained.

"We can't go back, Lucy, let's just enjoy that we are cousins and remember, we were friends first," Liselle reminded.

"You're right," Lucy agreed. "Fighting with Frieda isn't worth it. I will do what I think is best and I won't discuss this with her again. And Liselle . . ."

"Yes?"

"If I forget and get in a free-for-all with her, will you please stop me?"

"Oh, Lucy, you won't forget!"

～

The next few days Liselle worked at the restaurant while Lucy continued to pour over old microfiche at the library in an attempt to find information on the Cottingtons. She was coming up with nothing and realized with the approaching holidays she would have to put her search on hold.

～

A week later Lucy and Liselle sat on the veranda enjoying the last of the fall weather before the winter rains, discussing their favorite topic: childhood; each raised so differently from the other.

Many times Lucy caught herself comparing Liselle to Grandmother and wondering at the uncanny resemblance. She knew she resembled Grandfather McGivens, her love of the sea came from him and pictures confirmed that she had his short stocky build. For as long as she could recall, she imagined him riding the deck of his ship with great ease, his square solid body in sync with the waves.

"And what about your parents," Liselle asked. "Did they like living on Anderson?"

"Not really, my mother was a Seattle socialite and preferred the mainland. I don't think she really cared about Grandmother's house. They died in a boating accident a few years ago, but they hadn't lived on the island for years."

Liselle reflected on this; she and Lucy shared even the loss of parents, an extended family.

The evening had turned chilly and they gathered their things to go in when Lucy noticed a car turning down their lane. "Are we expecting anyone?"

"Not that I know of; who do you suppose it is?"

Lucy went to tell Emily to prepare hot cider while Liselle peered through the gathering dusk at the approaching car. She could just make out the outline of a sports car but not the driver. Moments later, a tall well-dressed young man with dark hair and eyes approached with brief case in hand.

"Miss Wintersted?" he inquired.

"Yes." She stood and smoothed her skirt.

"I'm Tom Caribou, I believe my office notified you I would be handling your estate matter," he flashed a warm smile as he climbed the stairs and held out his hand.

She flushed at the intensity of his gaze and looked down as he took her hand. "Yes, of course, won't you sit?"

"Forgive my intrusion, but since I was driving back from Alaska, I thought I would drop off some papers for your review. I hope my stopping is not inconvenient."

"Not at all, I appreciate your bringing these. Would you like some hot cider?" She hastened to add.

"Love some!"

Lucy reappeared with Emily carrying a tray of steaming mugs and fresh gingerbread, Liselle relieved by the interruption. She hadn't expected her new attorney to be close to her age or so attractive. It felt like he was memorizing her, the way he stared.

Introducing Lucy and Emily, she noticed again his warm smile as he stood to greet them, felt a quick flutter each time he looked at her.

After he left, Lucy leaned over. "Oh, my, he's quite the charmer. I saw the way he looked at you. If I were younger, I'd give you a run for this one!"

"Oh, Lucy, don't be ridiculous. I'm definitely not interested in any romance right now."

"Yeah, uh-huh, that's what they always say before they fall," she giggled.

~

Over the next two weeks, Tom Caribou called four times to update Liselle on each minute detail of her property transfer. Each time she hung up, she was convinced that he could have sent the information by letter or at least in one phone call.

On the Sunday before Thanksgiving Tom called as she and Lucy sat down to dine.

"Hi Liselle, I won't keep you but I'm free for the holiday and wondered if I might take you out to dinner or a movie?"

"Oh, that's very sweet, but Lucy and I are planning a dinner party." The minute the words were out, she regretted them, Thanksgiving was a time for family and friends and hastily she added: "Why don't you join us? There's always room for one more!"

He hesitated a second, "If you're sure I'm not imposing?"

"No, of course not, please come."

"All right, I'll be there early afternoon?"

"We'll see you then." Hanging up and returning to the dinner table, she realized that she much preferred having other people around when he was near. While his aggressive personality intrigued her, it also brought out her cautious side. He made her feel like a schoolgirl and she wondered if it was because he was an attorney while her interests gravitated toward the arts.

At any rate, when the documents were finalized and the property recorded, she was sure that would be the end of him, though she wondered why an attractive man like him was seemingly unattached.

12

THANKSGIVING DAWNED CRISP AND clear, a light snow predicted for that weekend. Recently Liselle had spent more nights at the mansion than her cottage, walking to the cottage each morning to check on it before she caught the ferry to work. Or she borrowed Lucy's van, as she had this morning.

On several occasions Lucy had invited her to move into the mansion but Liselle had refused; her attachment to the cottage strong. The place where her father had dreamed his dreams; maybe she would never actually live there, but now she dreamed her dreams. Perhaps it would be a summer getaway for the children she hoped to have some day.

As she turned into the driveway and glanced at the cottage, something seemed amiss and crossing the porch she glanced at the side yard, with a start realized the little apple tree was gone. She sprinted down the stairs for a closer inspection. Someone had chopped the tree down. Boot prints led from the yard up the muddy road in the direction of the cemetery.

Turning back to the house, it was then she noticed the shed. Next to Grant's wreath a terse warning had been painted: *now the apple tree—next time the rest—leave.*

She hesitated, torn between checking the house or getting in the van and driving away. Placing her key in the lock, she pushed open the door and breathed a sigh of relief. The rooms were as she had left them.

Tomorrow she would repaint the shed and move back to Lucy's. Perhaps that would satisfy whoever was attempting to evict her, yet send a message that she didn't scare easily.

$\approx$

The mansion was bustling with activity when Liselle returned, Emily basting turkeys, Cecelia and Nyls hanging garlands of greenery, the local youth polishing silver and setting tables. Liselle loved the dining room with its warm wood paneling and forest green wallpaper and busied herself making centerpieces for the tables, twisting holly and pinecones together with a cranberry candle in each center.

Soon Lucy came to check on her progress and together they admired the room.

"You seem quiet Liselle, are you nervous about Tom?"

"Oh, Tom; actually I had forgotten about him!"

Lucy looked dubious. "What happened to make you forget?"

"There was more vandalism at the house, I want to . . ."

"What kind of vandalism?" Lucy demanded.

"Someone chopped down the apple tree, so I want to . . ."

"I thought that was over. You need to move in here."

"I know! That's what I'm trying to say: I want to move in here . . ."

"Good, let's get your stuff tomorrow," Lucy began.

"There's something else."

Lucy turned to her with an expectant look.

"They spray painted the shed," Liselle explained.

"Not over the wreath, I hope?"

"No, thank God, they left that alone, but tomorrow I'll go over and repaint, get rid of the graffiti. I will move but I won't let them think they can mess up my property and I will just leave it that way."

The energy and excitement in the house, the aroma of food and flowers had put Liselle in a festive mood and she went to change for dinner. Selecting a sweater of pale blue mohair with a matching slim wool skirt, mother always said the color made her eyes look as deep as the ocean on a stormy day. Twisting her hair into a French braid and weaving a pale blue ribbon throughout, she added opal earrings and paused to study her reflection in the mirror. Soft curls framed her face and her skin glowed. Lucy was good for her!

Her first holiday without mother, she reflected on how much she had to be thankful for. What had started off as a very bad year now looked promising with friends and family. Tom, she decided, was not going to intimidate her.

She heard laugher as she approached the dining room and heads turned when she entered. Lucy, her cheeks matching her red velvet dress and eyes sparkling like a thousand diamonds on Lake Chelan, hurried to her side.

"Liselle, you look marvelous!" In a whisper, she added, "Tom's here!"

"Thank you, but I don't plan to spend all my time with him!"

"Even so, he's asking for you."

Just then Tom appeared.

"Hello, Liselle, would you like some cider?" he inquired.

"Yes, thank you," she took the glass and gazed into his intense dark eyes. "It was nice you could come."

"Thank you for inviting me. Otherwise I would probably just work," he explained, "but not on your matter, that's nearly wrapped."

"Good, that's one less thing I have to worry about."

"And what worries could you possibly have in that beautiful head," he asked.

She stared at him, not sure what to think of his remark and crossed her arms over slim breasts as she arched an eyebrow.

His charm not working, he cleared his throat and tried again. "Is there anything else I can help with?" he inquired.

"There may be," she paused, "I'll have to think about it. I believe dinner is being served." She moved to the nearest table and he hurried to seat her. As she introduced him to the other guests, several of whom she had met at church, she noticed the younger women eyeing him. Fine with me, she thought, they're probably more his type.

She tried to ignore Libby who sat across from them attempting to engage Tom in conversation while he continued talking to Liselle. It reminded her of a three-ring circus and she stifled the urge to giggle while an amused smile hovered around her lips. The wine was excellent and she began to relax just as Tom asked what she was planning to do the next day.

She answered without thinking, "Repainting my shed."

"You mean the property being deeded to you?" he inquired.

"Yes."

"Seems an odd time to paint?"

She bit her lip, having given more information than intended. Before she could answer, Libby happily volunteered the information. "Oh, Tom, everyone knows that someone vandalized the old Wintersted place!"

"What sort of vandalism?" his eyes narrowed as he ignored Libby.

"Just the usual, you know, vandalism," Liselle explained. "A little paint will fix it."

"It's my job to ask questions. This might be something you shouldn't ignore," he began.

"Yes, I know, but I'm at a loss over what to do." She surprised herself with her admission.

"That's what you have me for," he offered. "Do you mind if I look at it first?"

"No, I guess not," she heard herself saying, knowing this would not be the end of him and realizing she enjoyed his company.

"Why don't you pick me up tomorrow morning around 8:00 and we'll go over there," she invited.

"It's a deal," he said.

After dinner, they gathered in the den for a taffy pull, Liselle and Tom on opposite ends and laughing with the others. He was fun and his attention, if genuine, was what she secretly desired.

As the rest of the guests were leaving, he collected his jacket, too. "Miss Lucy," he said taking her hand, "thank you for today. I've had a wonderful time and you were the belle of the ball."

Lucy beamed a radiant smile to his warm grin.

~

The next morning Liselle was cruising through the home section of the newspaper when Cecelia entered the kitchen. "You have a visitor," she said with Tom in tow.

Even in old jersey and faded blue jeans he made her heart race. As he swept back a lock of unruly hair, she noticed his finely tapered hands.

"Good morning," she greeted.

"Good morning yourself," he responded. "You look just as lovely in the morning."

"Oh," she pushed a stray hair from her face.

"Actually, the newsprint across your nose is a nice touch," he teased.

Excusing herself, she raced on stocking feet to the powder room to dab at her face and returned with jacket and boots to find him having coffee with Emily.

"I'm ready when you are," she said.

"Here, sugar, take some coffee with you," Emily handed her a thermos.

"Thanks, Emily, tell Lucy to come over," she called to her.

In his sports car they drove the short distance to the cottage, Liselle relieved to see it still standing and nothing else bothered. On the way she told him about the vandalism of the cottage windows, but omitted mentioning the mirror in Grandmother's room.

While he photographed the shed, tree stump and footprints and inspected the cottage, she started a fire in the Franklin.

"You know that message: *'now the apple tree, next time the rest, et cetera'* doesn't look like a childish prank to me," he mused out loud and glanced at her.

She said nothing.

"Well, let's get started with that paint."

"You don't have to help," she offered.

"Of course I have to help. How often do I get to rescue a damsel in distress and this is definitely above and beyond the call of duty."

"In that case, please," she handed him a paintbrush. "I would like to see if you can handle this thing!"

"I used to do this all the time as a kid," he explained.

"Oh really and where was that?"

"In Alaska, I'm Aleut," he answered.

"A what . . ."

"Aleut, Aleutian from the Aleutian Islands, our language group Unangan is related to Eskimo. I've painted my share of boats, too. They were about this shade of gray, but we also had skin kayaks, called baidarkas," he explained.

"Well I'm happy to have such expert help because it's chilly out here and I'll be ready for a fire soon."

Tom began painting at the top corner while Liselle marked off a rainbow design to cover the graffiti. Working together it took less than an hour to finish.

Standing back, he appraised her art work. "You're not bad with that paint brush yourself," he teased. "We could have some snazzy fishing boats in Alaska, if you lived there!"

"It's too cold on this island," she responded, "forget about Alaska! Let's get some of Emily's coffee."

She put another log in the stove as Tom settled on floor cushions to watch her.

"I'm curious, Tom, tell me about this language group. That's a phrase I would expect to hear from an anthropologist, not an attorney."

"I suppose it is a little esoteric for the average lawyer, but I studied linguistics as an under-grad. Unangan meaning 'people of the shore' is my language of birth. I learned English in the mission school since our native tongue was not allowed to be spoken there. My mother is Russian, which we usually spoke at home."

"So why study linguistics?"

"I'm fascinated by the structure of language, and of course in the legal profession language is my tool of trade," he explained.

She was impressed with this intense, handsome man. The more she was around him, the more she discovered, like peeling an onion, each layer revealing another layer, until the core was reached. And what would his core reveal?

"You know, you don't look like a native," she said.

"And which native would that be," he teased, "the Aleuts, so named by the Russians, arrived there some 3,000 years before, or the Russians who arrived a few hundred years ago?"

"So what city," she asked, the history buff in her curious, "did you grow up?"

"Oh, it's not a city," he explained. "But St. Paul is the largest Aleutian community."

He smiled at her. "I don't want to hurry off, but I do need to check with my office," he said. "Do you have a phone I could use?"

"No phone, but we could go back to Lucy's and use hers," she offered.

On the way, he again cautioned. "About this vandalism, I don't think you should stay here alone, it's not a good idea."

"I agree and I'm moving in with Lucy for awhile."

"Good, glad to hear it. I don't want to leave, but I need to get back."

"Oh, I've kept you from something important . . ."

"I have to be in court Monday and still have several briefs to review. Can I call you next week?"

"Yes, I'd like that. You can reach me at Lucy's."

Liselle was sorry to see him go. When he turned his attention on her, she felt valued, as though everything she said was immensely important. No one had made her feel that way except her mother, and of course Lucy. Certainly no man ever had.

As he drove away, she turned to Lucy. "I expected you would come and join us."

"No," Lucy advised. "I would just be in the way. Why did Tom leave so soon?"

"He has briefs to review; said he would call next week."

"Yes, I imagine he will. You are glowing, you know!"

"Am I?!" Liselle's hands flew to her flushed face. "He is a very nice man, though I can't imagine what he sees in me."

"Well I know what he sees," Lucy offered, "a very attractive, clever and oh-so-caring young woman with a mind of her own. Some men like that, some don't. In my opinion, the smart one goes for the woman who thinks for herself."

"Lucy, you flatter me too much! Let's have lunch, I'm starved!"

And Liselle led the way to the kitchen.

13

LISELLE TRIED NOT TO appear anxious that week as each day came and went with no call from Tom, not even to update her on the deed. By Thursday she was in a bad mood. Work was boring, she didn't have the tiny cottage to look after since she had moved out for who knows how long, and she imagined that she had made a complete fool of herself to think that an incredibly bright, handsome attorney could possibly be interested in her. At her age she was practically an old maid and certainly would have been considered such a hundred years ago.

She was back to square one, with no place to go and no one to go there with, her bad attitude only making it worse. And it was the first anniversary of her mother's final illness. Last autumn the bad news had come, the next few months a blur with a bittersweet Christmas, for by then they had known it would be Ellen's last.

In an attempt to cheer Liselle, Lucy had taken her antique shopping in Snohomish and Poulsbo and attended the tree lighting ceremony in Steilacoom. By now the excitement of those had also faded, to be stored away with memories of other happier times.

Curious about Tom's background, Liselle immersed herself in studying the history of the Pribilof Islands and discovered they once were the seals' breeding ground; hunting them forbidden except for the natives to subsistence harvest.

"Will I ever see those islands," she mused, wondering if they were still so primitive for Tom seemed a classy and accomplished man. Nevertheless it was a new place to learn about and mentally she defended her research as a casual interest.

≈

Lucy was involved with guild and their annual toy drive; each morning they rode the ferry together as Lucy dropped Liselle at the cafe before continuing on to Kent. Each evening when Lucy picked her up and they rode the ferry back, Liselle grew more distant as Lucy chatted about her day, what she did, who she saw, what she had for lunch.

On Friday evening, Liselle snapped. "Lucy, if you tell me one more time what you had for lunch, I will scream," she blurted.

Lucy stopped mid-sentence. "Whatever is the matter with you?"

"I don't want to know what you had for lunch!"

"Okay, I'm sorry!"

They finished the trip in silence, Lucy glancing from time to time at Liselle's stormy profile where she sat as though carved in stone. After an equally silent dinner, Liselle went to her room while Lucy curled up with a mystery novel in the den.

~

Soon Liselle returned. "I've been acting foolishly, Lucy, to let anything come between us. I'm sorry for snapping at you, will you forgive me?"

"Of course, dear; sometimes I don't stop and think when I'm rambling on about nothing."

"It's not that," Liselle explained, "it's just that Tom was fun, he made me happy, not that you don't. He was just different."

"Of course he's different," Lucy agreed. "That's the way God intended it."

"Oh, Lucy, I don't mean like that," Liselle objected. "Not hearing from him this week, I feel like I'm back in limbo again, like I'm not going anywhere. I can't even live in the cottage, my job is boring . . ."

"What is your occupation?" Lucy asked.

"I studied graphic design and had just taken my first job with an advertising firm when Mother got sick."

"I should have known it had something to do with creativity," Lucy exclaimed.

"Maybe that's what I need right now, to create something," Liselle agreed. "Every year mother and I would make something special for Christmas. I didn't do that last year since she was sick . . . and died this past spring."

Liselle was deep in thought. "Lucy, you've lost your parents. How did you cope with that, both of them at once?"

"Len was my rock; he always tried to find the silver lining in every-thing which I sometimes found annoying. You know those old sayings don't always work for everything."

"That's true," Liselle agreed. "*In everything give thanks* is equally dif-ficult at the time you're going through it."

"Len kept me busy at holidays and that was a good thing because even though my parents came to visit, I sometimes felt like I was an afterthought to them!"

Liselle smiled. "That's what I need, to stay busy, make something, a Christmas memory and I think I know just what that is!"

She raced to her room and returned with a shoe box.

"Lucy, how about it, our first Christmas and we can make something together, what do you say?"

"Oh I don't know, I always buy things, I've never had the patience."

"Come on, I'll show you, it isn't difficult. You do save your Christmas cards, birthday cards, things like that?" Liselle asked.

"Of course, I could never throw those out!"

"Great! Bring the ones that are special, and we'll make a Christmas collage."

At her hesitation, Liselle encouraged, "it will be fun; I keep my cards in this box."

~

When Lucy returned with several boxes of old cards, Liselle had al-ready begun her layout and glancing up, she smiled at Lucy.

"Pick one card with a theme and lay others around it with the same idea. These cards are from my last Christmas with mother. I chose a dove with the word *peace*. Now I select other cards with doves and peace and then I cut the cards . . ."

"You *cut* your cards?" Lucy was incredulous.

"Yes, but you don't have to. You can use the entire card, just overlap the edges. Or use these specialty scissors for a pretty edge. Then we will decoupage . . ."

Lucy started slowly, selecting Christmas cards that Len had given her over the years and as she gathered momentum her collage began to take shape. Carefully she trimmed with scissors as Liselle began talking.

"You know, my mother was somewhat of a maverick," she said.

"Really," Lucy was surprised. "I had the impression that Ellen was very prim and proper."

"Not at all," Liselle assured. "Maybe because she was raised by two elderly people who doted on an only child, as they did me. Mother was pretty but headstrong. She studied Art History and enjoyed music, travel, dressed Bohemian at times, and wore her hair really long. I have pictures of me holding onto her braids when we hiked. She started me early and we continued to hike right up until the summer before she died."

Lucy listened intently as she worked on her collage. It was the first time Liselle had really opened up and talked about her mother.

"Your collage is really beautiful, Lucy," Liselle complimented.

Lucy smiled. "There are wonderful memories here, thank you for showing me this."

Just then Emily entered with bowls of popcorn.

"You have a call, Miss Liselle."

"Thanks, Emily."

"Hi Liselle, it's Tom; sorry I didn't call sooner but I was stuck at the office late every night. I really apologize. The papers are ready for your signature. Can I bring them up Saturday?"

"Oh, Tom, that's too much trouble, just drop them in the mail and I will find a notary here," Liselle responded.

"It's no trouble," he insisted. "I really want to bring them."

She wasn't sure she wanted to see him again, now that she had decided he wasn't interested. She might change her mind and get her hopes up again. Saying "no" felt much safer.

"I don't know if that's a good idea," she began.

"I've missed you. I had a good time at Thanksgiving," he added.

She softened, remembering how he had shared that day at the cottage.

"Well, all right, if you really want to drive all that way just to get my signature, I suppose I can say yes," she said.

"Great! I'll be there around noon tomorrow."

Lucy didn't look up when Liselle returned, keeping her head down to hide the grin that spread across her face.

After a few moments, she cleared her throat. "Liselle, why do you stay at that job?"

"What do you mean?"

"You don't have to work at the restaurant. You own the Wintersted place so no rent is due. You can live here as long as you want, so why don't you do something you like. And if you feel you owe me room and board, you can work in the garden with Nyls. I know you'd rather do that than be in the kitchen!"

"Oh, I don't mind helping in the kitchen, in fact I could learn some things from you and Emily—but working with Nyls, now there's a thought! I'd like to try and crack what's in his mind, he's a strange one."

As they nibbled popcorn, Liselle thought about the idea.

"You know, Lucy, I'm going to do it! Quit the restaurant. On Monday I'll give Jana two weeks' notice, it's off season now."

"Good! I think you need to stop wasting time waiting tables. You've had a lot of change this year and you deserve a really nice Christmas. Same for me, since Len died I haven't really done Christmas. This is the first time that I actually feel like celebrating. You can join guild, too, if you like."

"Thanks, but the guild is not for me, at least not yet. I'd much rather work with Nyls, see what's cooking under that floppy little hat of his. I think I'll start tomorrow on my day off."

~

The next morning Liselle decided to investigate the tool shed while she waited for Nyls to arrive. In winter he didn't start before mid-morning. She was surprised to find the shed locked and strode to the kitchen to find Emily drinking a cup of coffee.

"Emily, do you know where Nyls keeps the keys to the tool shed?"

"Well, yes, now sugar, they're right here, but Nyls don't like someone messing around his stuff," she cautioned.

"Oh, I'm not messing around, Emily, I'm his new assistant; it will be fine."

Returning to the shed, she unlocked the door and slid it sideways, the dank smell of compost rising to greet her as she stepped across the threshold. Walking past rows of chemicals she read the names on the cans: rose fertilizer, aphid spray, ant spray, pruning paste, black paint–*black* paint! What was that doing here?

She picked up the can and gave it a shake, finding it nearly empty. Could it be? Slipping the can into an old plastic bag, she felt like a detective. Perhaps fingerprints could be taken; she would ask Tom when he arrived.

A shadow fell across the doorway.

"Tom! What are you doing here?"

"I believe I was invited!"

"You were; you're early!"

"And you're as lovely as I remember!" he teased.

"Go away," she said, "I think you keep popping up to catch me off-guard!"

"That's part of my charm," he said, "and so far I haven't been disappointed! What are you up to out here?"

"I found black spray paint in the gardener's shed! Do you suppose fingerprints can be taken?"

"And prove what? That the gardener used that can of paint? I'm sure you'll find his fingerprints all over it. This is his shed. That won't tie him to the vandalism at your property, unless of course this is the only can of black spray paint on the island and . . ."

"You're teasing me!"

"Yes, I am, sorry. It seems like a good idea but there's no proof that this spray paint was ever at your place, fingerprints won't prove that!"

"Okay, I retire as super sleuth," she began and looked up to see Nyls standing in the doorway, glaring at her.

"Miss Wintersted, this is my shed, while working for me, do not snoop around," he commanded.

"Yes, sir, I was just getting an early start," she answered meekly.

"Not here," he snapped.

She backed out of the shed followed by Tom and they raced to the kitchen.

"Nice guy," said Tom.

"Yeah," she agreed, "actually I don't think he quite realizes yet that he works for me!"

They both laughed. "And how does he work for you?"

"Oh, Lucy and I are cousins, didn't you know?" she asked.

But Tom's legal mind was already turning over the possibility that Nyls might very well have something to hide; his rudeness seemed out of place. He decided to order a background check on Nyls when he returned to his office.

After Liselle signed the documents, Tom notarized them and they had lunch in the kitchen with Emily. A drizzling rain had started and he wanted to get back before it turned to freezing.

Walking together to his car, he plotted when he might see her again. With his hand on the door, he turned to her.

"I want to take you out over the Christmas holiday."

"Oh, you do!"

"Yes, I don't know what your plans are, but I want to spend Christmas Eve with you."

"Lucy has her Christmas gala and I was planning a quiet evening at home."

"Then let's go to Seattle for dinner, maybe a show, whichever you prefer."

"You decide."

"I'll pick you up at 4:00."

"Okay . . ."

Her reply was cut short as he pulled her close and brushed his lips against her forehead. She drew back and looked into his eyes. When he encircled her with his arms she didn't resist. He kissed her on the lips, then released her and opened his car door.

"I'll call you next week!"

Liselle watched his taillights disappear and noticed the drizzle had turned to snow; the delicate flakes softening the pounding of her heart. She walked inside to find Lucy in the hallway holding her jacket.

"I was just about to come and get you!"

"He wants to take me out Christmas Eve!"

"Wonderful!" Lucy beamed at the news. "I can't imagine that he wouldn't!"

Tom called when he found time; Lucy occupied with last minute details for the Charity Ball while Liselle gave Jana two weeks' notice, then concentrated on Christmas. She went with Lucy to Guild, met some of her friends and shopped before returning home.

14

EARLY ONE MORNING SHE drove Lucy to the ferry so she and Cecelia could decorate the house. When she finished, she thought of her little cottage, once again dark and abandoned. Lucy had plenty of decorations and wouldn't mind if she decorated her cottage, too.

As she drove, she realized she hadn't been back since the day she and Tom had repainted the shed. How perfect the little apple tree would have looked with mini-lights. Instead she strung lights on the small pine near the front steps and along the roof's edge.

Running an extension cord to the shed, she strung lights around it, too, and hung a fresh holly wreath over Grant's painted wreath. For the finishing touch she placed a nativity set on the front porch; then paused to admire her work, unaware that someone watched her from across the road. She hoped whoever had left the hostile messages would leave this alone. It was Christmas!

Placing the empty boxes in Lucy's car, it was then she saw the envelope beneath the seat. Jackson's letter! Tattered, stained, and mangled, she managed to read the words written several months ago.

Lisy,

don't know where you are; hope this finds you. Sorry about your loss, but like I said, life goes on. Call me so we can get together.

Jack

Wow, she tossed his letter and drove away. She had barely thought about him and now she knew why. He hadn't been there for her, even though his mother died. They should have been able to share experiences;

instead he had acted like it wasn't a life-changing shake you up event. And she hated the nickname he insisted on calling her.

She breathed a sigh of relief that he didn't have her address and filed him under one less complication. With a week to Christmas, she needed to shop for Tom. What did handsome attorneys like?

∾

Tom left his office early to shop for Liselle. Undoubtedly the most interesting woman he had met, with a sweetness he found lacking in other women, with her he felt grounded, having finally realized he was tired of the dating game. And her looks!

But she was more than a pretty face for he had fallen in love with her, wanted to spend his life with her.

Entering the exclusive jewelry store, he placed his order with the elegant, perfumed clerk who commandeered the counter. Leaving a hefty deposit, he stuffed the receipt in his briefcase and hurried back to the office. As he sat down, his secretary buzzed him.

"You have a lady visitor, she didn't give her name."

"Send her in," he said, thinking of Liselle. It took a moment to remember the young blond who strolled in. They had met at an office party at Halloween; she worked across the street at another law firm.

"Uh—Jenny, how are you?"

She flashed her most charming smile and giggled. "Worried, Tom, I haven't seen you in forever," she explained.

"Well, you know the life of a lawyer," he explained.

"Of course, but we needn't let that get in the way of love," she countered.

"Whoa, Jenny, I never said anything about love," he paled.

She went from flirty to mad in zero seconds. "You certainly acted like it!"

"You can't just drop by in the middle of the day, I'm very busy."

"When you don't call, Tom, what am I supposed to do," she chided; then softened her approach and changed the subject. "What are we doing for Christmas?"

"I have plans," he explained.

"Without me . . ."

"Yes, I have another engagement."

"What about us," she began.

"There is no 'us', Jenny. You really need to move on, I think," he tried to let her down easy, but she wasn't going for it and tears pooled in her eyes.

Excusing himself, he went to his secretary.

"Get her out of here," he said. "I'm gone for the rest of the day."

His secretary rolled her eyes at his retreating back and picked up a box of Kleenex, another perk in the life of a legal secretary.

15

It was Christmas Eve and Lucy was in a state of panic. "Liselle, I can't find my fur, where did Cecelia put it! Oh, this is a disaster! I can't find my other heel; I shouldn't be going without an escort."

"Lucy, calm down, you'll get a migraine. Sit still so I can fix your hair. I will find your shoe. Cecelia, please get her chinchilla from the cedar closet!"

"Liselle, I don't know about this dress. I shouldn't have let you talk me out of my black and pearls. I won't be comfortable in this!"

The strapless gown of emerald taffeta showcased her creamy shoulders, the high waist flaring to a bell skirt that skimmed sequined shoes, the diamond necklace and earrings a last gift from Len.

"You look elegant. Will you stop worrying; you'll probably come home with three beaus."

"I doubt if Frieda will let that happen!"

Lucy loved this time of year when everyone dressed in their finest and spent the evening dancing, but it was her first without Len and she was nervous tagging along with Frieda and her husband, Karl.

"Liselle, you need to get ready. I don't want you to be late for your big evening!"

"We've been over this a hundred times, Lucy, you're leaving first and I have plenty of time! Besides, I wanted to give you this," she handed her an oblong box tied with a velvet ribbon.

"What is it?" Lucy tore off the ribbon and opened the box, exclaiming with delight as she removed a narrow gold bracelet with the letter "L" in rhinestones. Liselle held up her wrist to display its twin.

"You are your grandmother's granddaughter!"

"It seemed appropriate, somehow," Liselle explained as they laughed and hugged.

Cecelia returned with Lucy's wrap and announced the arrival of Frieda and Karl, the three of them planning to spend the night in Kent, returning on the morning ferry.

Liselle kissed Lucy and saw her out the door.

～

Alone, Liselle returned to her room, still debating what to wear. She decided on her basic black and pearls. Lucy would never go for something so plain, especially since she had talked her out of wearing hers, but she definitely wanted to be comfortable tonight.

Sweeping her hair back, she fastened it with pearl combs, a gift from her grandparents. Her hair feathered softly around her face while the length fell in loose curls down her back.

Earlier she had phoned her grandparents and they had wept upon hearing her say she was grateful for them telling her about the adoption, because they loved her and had taught her the importance of family, had instilled in Ellen the values passed down to her. The only grandparents she would ever know, she updated them on what she had learned about Elizabeth and they were happy her search had been successful.

Her Grandfather's plea touched her heart. "We never told your mother because it seemed unfair to give her so many unanswered questions. I hope you can forgive us."

"Gipa," she said, "I understand better now how hard it was; the fear of losing her. And you taught me forgiveness."

～

The doorbell rang and she heard Cecelia answer. Picking up her leather coat she walked to the foyer. On seeing her, Tom flashed a smile and hurried to hold her coat while she wrapped a silk scarf around her neck and pulled on leather gloves.

"Liselle, you look wonderful!"

"Thank you," she grinned mischievously. "You don't look so bad yourself!"

A bright red scarf over his black trench gave him a debonair look, the cold having brought a flush to his cheeks. His dark eyes sparkled and his aftershave hovered in the air to stir strange sensations in her.

"Ready?" he asked, reaching for the door.

"Yes, good night, Cecelia; Merry Christmas!"

"Merry Christmas to you both," Cecelia replied.

Tom had left the engine running and they sat in the car for the ferry ride across the bay. When he reached for her gloved hand, she again caught the fragrance of his aftershave. He smelled divine and all her senses were in overdrive.

"You don't need gloves you know." She removed them to discover a warm hand squeezing hers. "Does this mean you have a warm heart?" she inquired, smiling at him.

"Absolutely!!" he grinned back. She didn't know where this relationship would lead but as hard as she tried, she couldn't imagine he was serious about her. She also couldn't imagine a future without him and felt irresistibly drawn to his warmth, his charisma, like a flower to the sun.

"Where are we going?" she asked.

"I have reservations for dinner at the Space Needle."

"Oh wonderful, I haven't been there in years!"

He found a parking spot near the Needle and they rode the glass elevator 500 feet to the top, their table by the window providing a panoramic view of Seattle as the restaurant rotated.

She relaxed as he began to talk about his work. It was obvious he loved the law, though it was a hard taskmaster requiring long hours and offering little thanks as it consumed his time. But he seemed to thrive on it and was beginning to build a steady clientele.

"This is special, Tom."

"I concur!"

She laughed at how easily he slipped into legalese. When she pointed this out, he joined in laughter. "Actually," he continued, "this is my favorite restaurant when I'm in Seattle. You can view the entire city in an hour."

"I probably knew that," she agreed. "I used to love coming here by trolley, mother and I, riding from Westlake Center and on to Pike Place!" Memories of Ellen no longer caused such pain and now she could speak of her easily. "Of course, we made a day of it and usually squeezed in the Art Museum."

"I rode the trolley once to the Kingdome," he agreed, "but I prefer to drive. My car is a blast; maybe I'll let you take it for a spin some day."

"You're on," she said.

Their entrees cooked to perfection, Tom entertained her with stories of different clients. She listened with delight, laughing easily at his exaggerated descriptions.

"I was probably your most boring client?"

"Only from the standpoint of how easy your file was, open and shut. On a personal level, I would have to say you are anything but boring!"

She blushed at the unexpected compliment as the heart she so carefully guarded now careened into new territory and she sought a different topic to discuss.

"Something has puzzled me since the first time you stopped at Lucy's."

"And what's that," he smiled.

"On your return from Alaska, you drove out of your way to meet me."

"Oh," he chuckled out loud. "When Joseph's 'old' clients were being parceled out, I told Peggy I only wanted the young, pretty ones! I thought I was being funny, but she obliged and gave me your file. She said you definitely qualified."

Liselle felt the blush spread from her neck to the roots of her hair and Tom laughed harder as she joined him.

"So, of course, I had to see for myself," he finished, enjoying the color in her face.

With her defenses down, he smiled as his eyes hungrily drank in her features, her wide full lips and perfect teeth, mahogany hair that softly feathered away from her face, the straight nose with a slight Grecian look. And eyes that hinted of deep passion as they changed from the ocean on a sunny day to dark and stormy when troubled.

There was nothing hidden about her, except perhaps her caution with men, with him. She was a challenge and one he was eager to take on. Being with her, he felt as if he had finally come home.

～

After cappuccinos they stood outside on the observation deck where he slipped his arm around her, having waited patiently for this moment. The city lights twinkled below and Puget Sound lie somewhere beyond in the inky blackness.

"Liselle, are you cold, do you want to go back inside?"

"No, this is really beautiful; I'm not ready to go in."

They stood at the rail and gazed into the stillness.

"If you don't mind the cold," he began, "maybe you'd like to visit Alaska some day?"

"I've always wanted to and you make it sound fascinating!"

"I mean with me."

She stared at him, "With you?!"

"Yes, will you marry me?" He reached into his pocket and pulled out a small velvet box. Nestled on the black velvet lining was a diamond solitaire set on a slim gold band with matching sapphires on either side.

"Tom," she breathed as he slipped the ring on her finger, "it's beautiful, incredible."

"Like you—beautiful, different—a diamond for my love, the sapphires for your eyes."

"This is rather sudden!"

"Maybe; I only know that from the day we met, I've wanted to be with you!"

Her heart pounded wildly as she bent over the railing, long curls cascading forward to hide the emotion flooding her face. Was it possible? After all the losses, God had sent this incredible man into her life? She could only think of the most basic response.

"Where would we live?"

"In Olympia, of course, where my job is. If you want to go back to work you can, or stay home and take care of us. We'll buy a house; build a house, whatever you want. We can decide all that later. Only say yes and make me the happiest man in the world."

"I don't know what to say. I mean, I'm just, in . . . shock; didn't know you felt this way!"

He kissed her and she kissed him back.

"From the first time I saw you on Lucy's porch," he said, cradling her soft curls in his hand.

Heat spread through her and she was aware of his body pressed against her. She pulled away, shaken by the intensity of her response.

A relationship with a man was not something she took lightly. It had to be right, the timing, the shared values and goals.

"But you hardly know me!" she protested.

"It doesn't take long to figure out if someone is right and you are right for me, in so many ways," he argued.

She was silent.

"It's cold out here, perhaps we should go back inside," he said, puzzled at her silence.

At his look of dejection, she wrapped her arms around him.

"Our future happiness depends on us making the right decisions now."

"I don't have any doubt that you're the woman I want to marry."

He held the door for her and back at their table ordered hot chocolate.

"We haven't discussed religion or kids," she began. "Those issues are important to me."

"Fair enough," he agreed. "You know I attended the Orthodox Church and school."

"Yes, you told me; are you a Christian?"

"Of course I'm a Christian. I went to the mission school, for Pete's sake!"

"Church is important to me . . ." she explained.

"It is to me, too, but I don't go every Sunday. With my profession, Sundays can get folded right in with Saturdays when I have a big case to defend. As for kids, I have brothers and hope to have two or three kids some day."

Not sure they agreed on every critical issue, for the moment she was satisfied; her heart telling her she could be happy with him. Besides, it was Christmas Eve and she wanted to enjoy the evening.

"Is that enough examination for now?" he asked.

"Yes," she laughed. "No more interrogation on my part. However, any additional briefs you wish to submit will be greatly appreciated."

He chuckled at her choice of words and paying the tab, they rode the elevator to the ground. He was silent, his eyes dark pools of amber as he slipped his arm around her.

"I love you Liselle."

She snuggled into his warmth. "I love you . . . yes, I will marry you."

～

They caught the midnight ferry to Anderson and drove to her cottage. Ablaze with lights against a black winter sky, the place looked warm and cheery, a light snow having dusted the small pine by the porch. She imagined her father had loved it here.

"Merry Christmas," she said kissing his cheek. "I want to keep the cottage for a summer retreat."

"Sure," he said, absently, though he didn't really care much for the house. It was too small and decrepit, reminding of his youth. So far he had avoided places that evoked memories of such poverty.

"I almost forgot to give you your gift."

She pulled a small jeweler's box from her coat pocket. Surprised, he popped open the lid.

"Do you like them," she whispered, as he inspected the cufflinks set with Alaskan quartz, a chunky gold nugget in the center.

"Yes, very much, thank you," he said, kissing her.

He drove her back to Lucy's. To avoid gossip, which seemed to travel around the island at lightning speed, Liselle didn't offer him to spend the night, though there were many bedrooms in the mansion.

Saying good-night, he returned on the ferry to his hotel in Steilacoom. He would see her later on Christmas and they would announce their engagement. Lucy would be the first to know. Then he would return to Olympia for a big trial scheduled for January.

Even though it was a short trip across the Sound, he was weary of the ferry. Once they were married and settled in Olympia, his trips to the island would be few and far between, he decided.

~

The week between Christmas and New Year's passed quickly, Tom inviting Liselle to his firm's New Year's Eve celebration. She declined and offered instead they attend the dinner-dance hosted by Frieda. The biggest event of the year, the entire island would be there.

Liselle spent the week mulling over Tom's marriage proposal. Excited at the idea of marriage and a family of her own, her mind raced with plans for their future but they had yet to pick a date.

Not one to rush into things she listed the pros and cons of marrying Tom and moving back to Olympia. Mother would have liked him; a definite pro, but there was unfinished business here with the vandalism, a con.

And why did Grandmother give away her baby. Maybe the reason would never be known and she would have to be content with that, but the larger issue remained: someone wanted her out of the Wintersted place and something unsolved, perhaps dangerous, lingered to haunt her.

16

THE SKY WAS CLEAR on New Year's Eve as Liselle and Tom approached Frieda's house and they stared at the mansion ablaze with lights as beautiful music poured forth. Crossing the terrace to the entry, they left their coats with the butler and Tom guided Liselle into the ball room where crystal chandeliers glittered from the magnificent domed ceiling.

The orchestra began a waltz and Tom pulled Liselle close, whispering "Can't take my eyes off of you." She smiled at the Frankie Valli song, one of her favorites, aware of how striking they looked together.

Superb in his fitted tuxedo, with sparkling eyes and glossy black hair, Tom cut a grand figure on the dance floor as he held her close, her fiery hair and glowing skin showcased in a long gown of ocean blue velvet that mirrored the color of her eyes.

Tom's Christmas gift, a single strand of fiery crystal, followed the curve of her neck while the engagement ring with its sapphires flashed brilliantly on her hand.

He hugged her tightly and whispered, "Have I told you tonight how beautiful you are?"

"For only about the tenth time, but thank you, kind sir."

She gave a mock curtsey and twirled playfully in his arms. When the waltz ended, they walked to the lavish buffet designed to please the most discriminating gourmet.

Carefully balancing their plates, Tom led the way to the heated terrace and seated Liselle near a fountain. As he returned inside for their drinks Libby blocked his path.

"Hello, Mr. Gorgeous Attorney," she said.

"Libby, how are you tonight?"

"Why don't you dance with me and find out," she invited, slipping her arms around his neck.

"I'm busy right now," he said, "and I'm pretty sure my dance card is full." He smiled, "Excuse me."

He ducked out of her arms to leave her pouting. How easy to attract the wrong kind of woman, he mused; well, that was about to change.

Hugging her shawl about her, Liselle enjoyed the fountain's colored lights as they flashed in time with the music. Squinting, she thought she saw a figure on the lawn just at the edge of the trees.

"You shouldn't sit here alone!"

Startled, she turned to see a tall man of blond good looks standing before her. Dressed in a tuxedo that he wore with the casual air of someone who might go horse-back riding in the moonlight, he grinned at her.

"You just never know who might want to dance with you!" Boldly he thrust out his hand, "Geoff Harmeyer."

"Liselle Wintersted," she responded, extending her hand. In one smooth motion he bent over and brushed his lips across her hand.

"A lovely name, it fits you. I can see I have waited too long to meet you."

She felt her face color; thankful it was dark, not sure what to think of this handsome stranger. And what would Tom say if he found her talking to another man; an attractive one?

"Would you care to dance?"

"Thank you, but . . ."

"Excuse me, the lady is with me!" Tom had returned with drinks.

"Tom, this is Geoff Harmeyer; my fiance Tom Caribou. Geoff was just concerned about my being alone."

"Thank you for your concern, Geoff, I can take it from here."

Geoff winked at Liselle and retreated into the ballroom.

"It was bad judgment to leave you out here," Tom replied.

"There's no harm, he was just being friendly," she explained. "He is the son of our hostess."

"Uh-huh, and I just fell off a turnip truck," he scowled. "I brought coffee; perhaps we should go in."

"It's beautiful tonight, the way the moon glides across the sky, behind the pine trees and out again, the wispy clouds trailing behind. The beauty of God's creation never ceases to amaze me . . ."

Tom kissed her in mid-sentence. "Me either," he agreed as he wrapped his arms around her. "Let's go inside. The orchestra is starting to play some fast numbers and there will be more slow ones."

Liselle had forgotten about the shadow in the trees and didn't hear the crunch of twigs as they crossed the terrace. Entering the ballroom they came face to face with Frieda.

Frieda's icy eyes moved across Liselle from head to toe before she turned to Karl and surrounded by their friends, laughed heartily at something he said.

Turning away, Liselle saw Geoff dancing with Libby and wondered what Frieda would do if she had danced with Geoff. Before she could ponder that, the band leader stepped to the microphone.

"Ladies and gentlemen," he began. "Our first mixer is gentlemen's choice, just in case you ladies aren't sure who you want to dance with. I'm sure the fellows have it all figured out!"

Liselle blushed when she saw Geoff walking toward her with Libby in tow. "Now's your chance Tom," Libby giggled and with a gallant flourish, Tom held out his hand.

"Liselle?" Geoff held out his arm and she stepped into his circle as he pulled her close. When the dance finished, Liselle rejoined Tom and for the next mixer, Tom pulled her outside.

"I'm sorry but I won't share you again," he explained.

They danced on the terrace as the New Year became official and fireworks burst over their heads for Tom didn't plan to let Geoff kiss her either.

~

Back at Lucy's they changed into jeans and sweaters to curl up in front of the fireplace. The ferry ran late and Tom was driving back to Olympia that night.

Now he drew her close and she leaned against his shoulder, savoring his after shave. It was a comforting man-smell and she snuggled into his chest.

He sighed. "I can't stay too long, but I don't want to leave."

"I don't want you to leave, tonight has been wonderful!"

He kissed her cheek, nuzzled her neck and soft hair. She sat up and turned to face him. Serious eyes gazed at her and she placed her hands firmly on his arms.

"Tom, I love you and I know we need to pick a date . . ."

"That sounds like a 'but' is coming . . ." he began.

"Well, sort of, I need to finish things here, the vandalism. I can't move to Olympia yet."

"Why is that important to you, Liselle? We have our whole future to think about. Can't you let it go?"

"I can't," she defended.

"So far no one has gotten hurt!"

"And no one will," she argued. "Maybe I should give you back the ring."

"The ring is yours; no one else will ever wear it."

Tears welled in her eyes and she looked down, "I'm sorry I can't leave this alone. Try to understand?"

He paused before answering. "I am trying."

Tears spilled down her cheeks and gently he wiped them away.

"I'll be busy for a few weeks with the trial but I'll call every day. And I want you to be careful. You don't really know what or who you're up against here."

He had hoped she would move back to Olympia so he wouldn't have to worry. Now with no way to assess the situation the thought made him nervous.

"There's nothing I can say to change your mind," he tried one last time.

"I will stay with Lucy, and work with Nyls."

She walked him to the door and he bent to kiss her.

"Call me so I know you got home?" she asked. "It is New Year's Eve!"

"Sure."

Disappointment flooded him and walking quickly to his car, he hesitated before he walked back. Taking her firmly in his arms, he kissed her long and deeply. She stumbled when he released her.

～

A light fog hung over the interstate as Tom raced along deserted streets, most parties still going strong. The upcoming trial would keep him busy and for that he was grateful but at the moment he felt frustrated. He didn't like loose ends for even though Liselle wore his ring, Geoff was a loose end.

17

AFTER TOM LEFT, LISELLE sat by the fire watching the embers die as she pondered her decision. Would Tom wait? He said he would but then he hadn't tried very hard to change her mind. Had he lost interest?

A ring was a small price to pay to get out of a relationship he wasn't sure about. And what was his parting kiss designed to do? Break her down, change her mind, or was it good-bye?

What would mother say? She rubbed her forehead.

Be true to yourself, mother always said. At any rate, she had to continue her present course. She had come a long way this past year: from the devastation of her mother's death to finding her cousin, and now waking to a more powerful and different love for Tom. An exciting future awaited her; was she about to throw it all away by stubbornly pursuing some quest that might not matter very much?

The sound of a car engine ended her reverie; Lucy home early. Liselle slipped down the hall to Grandmother's bedroom and read before falling into fitful sleep.

Tom's call woke her.

"I'm back. I went to the club to work out; now I'm off to the office. What are you doing today?"

"I suppose just hanging out. I miss you!" Silence on the other end. "Tom, are you there?"

"Yes, I'm here. Call when you want to talk. I'm just disappointed."

"It won't be forever!"

"It feels like it!"

"Well, I promise it won't be forever."

"Okay, happy new year, Liselle, I love you."

"I love you too. God bless with the trial."

She hung up and went in search of Emily who was due back this morning. To her surprise, she was already in the kitchen making potato pancakes. Liselle had finished one stack before Lucy appeared with a puffy face.

"Morning Liselle, what happened with Tom last night?"

"We didn't set a date."

"What?" Lucy gaped at her.

"My goal is to get loose ends tied up here. I'm not ready to move back to Olympia which is where we would live."

"I didn't realize that," exclaimed Lucy. "I'm glad you aren't leaving, but what about Tom, will he wait?"

"I guess so. He said he would." They ate in silence for a few minutes. "I'm moving into my cottage . . ."

"You aren't serious!"

"It's the only way to draw the enemy's fire, find out who's behind the vandalism, why the threatening messages against me or the Wintersteds or whatever."

"Well, you shouldn't stay there alone!"

"If I have to live alone to get this done then I will!"

"Does Tom know you're doing this?"

"No, I didn't discuss it with him."

"And I can pretty much imagine why. You know what he would say."

"Tom and I aren't married. I owe him no explanation."

"When will you move?" Lucy asked resignedly.

"Tomorrow, but I will still work with Nyls. I have a hunch that something's going on with him in all of this."

"Nyls seems harmless to me!"

"Maybe, but you should have seen him when I went in his shed without permission!"

"What happened?"

"He keeps the shed locked so I got the keys from Emily. He found Tom and me in there and wasn't very nice about it!"

"How odd, nobody locks anything on this island, least of all a shed."

"That's what I thought!" Liselle agreed.

~

Mid-morning Liselle strolled to the shed to find Nyls bent over scrubbing pots.

"Morning Nyls, happy new year!"

He barely glanced at her.

"What would you like me to work on this week?" she asked.

"Well, now, I have to think on it some," he answered.

"When you figure it out, just leave a note on the greenhouse door; I won't be here early anymore," she explained.

"Oh, why's that?" he queried.

"I'll be coming from the cottage."

He rose then to face her. It was the first time he had actually looked at her and what she saw filled her with alarm, his eyes cold and filled with . . . malice? With her lanky build and he stooped with age, they were about the same height and staring into his face, she noticed purple veins crisscrossing his bulbous nose. Estimating him to be about her father's age, she wondered if they had known each other.

She didn't like the feeling he gave and suddenly weary of him, she turned and walked to the house.

❧

Later that afternoon she and Lucy loaded the van with the things she had gradually moved over. "I think you should consider having a telephone," Lucy said.

"If it won't cost too much, I suppose it would be convenient."

"Convenient . . . it will be safe! And I would feel a lot better. I still think you should have someone sleep over."

"I can't think of anyone besides you, Lucy, and you wouldn't be comfortable."

"Will you at least wait until the phone is in?" Lucy pleaded.

"It will be all right; I'll call the phone company first thing in the morning."

As they pulled into the driveway, Liselle noticed the nativity set missing from the porch and saying nothing, began walking to the steps. Her feet crunched something and looking down, let out a startled cry. Colored glass littered the ground; the Christmas lights all broken out of their sockets.

Lucy followed her as she unlocked the front door and stepped in. Everything as she left it, Liselle hurried through the kitchen and out the side door. The lights on the shed were smashed as well; the holly wreath lay trampled in the mud.

Lucy searched Liselle's face but she avoided looking at her. "Do you still insist on staying here?"

Liselle raised her chin, "Yes, I want this over. If my staying here will speed things up, then *so be it.*"

"Then I am moving a bed over and staying with you, at least until the phone is in."

After Lucy left, Liselle busied herself in the kitchen putting away groceries.

She jumped at the knock on her door and opened it to find Geoff standing there.

"Hey Liselle, I thought I saw you here," he explained, smiling.

"Can I help you?"

"Oh, I was just paying a good neighbor visit," he flashed a wider smile and she smiled back. He was a charmer.

"Please, come in," she held the door open and pulled open curtains as he stumbled across the threshold. In the pale light he looked chilled.

"Can I offer you coffee?" she asked.

"Actually, tea would be nice."

She walked to the kitchen and he followed.

"As you can see, the place is very small," she began.

"Oh, yes, I've been in here before!"

"You . . . have?" Liselle was surprised.

"Yes, the house was rarely locked, my buddies and I used to hang here."

"I see," she handed him a mug of steaming Earl Grey, poured one for her.

"Let's sit in the living room."

She moved to make a fire in the Franklin stove and he jumped to her side.

"Let me do that for you."

She handed him the matches and settled on cushions to study his sure movements and lean build. High cheekbones gave his face a sculptured look, his merry blue eyes and compelling smile so unlike Frieda.

"It should be warm in here soon," he promised.

"Okay, neighbor, and to what do I owe this visit?" she asked as he settled nearby.

"I felt bad about your little tree," carefully he sipped hot liquid.

"What about my tree?"

"Well, I shouldn't have done what I did, it was so . . ."

"What did you do?"

"I thought you knew it was gone!"

Her eyes opened wide. "You did that?"

"Yes, and it doesn't look the same without it."

"So it was a prank?" She couldn't believe it.

"What did you think?"

"I thought the message was scary and overdone for a prank!"

"What message?"

"The one you painted on my shed!"

"I didn't put any message on your shed; I chopped the tree and came to apologize."

"If you didn't leave a message who . . . ?"

"I don't know God's truth! I wouldn't do something like that. What was the message?"

She paused; someone had taken advantage of Geoff's mischief.

"Someone wants me out of this house, and I don't know why."

"Well, I don't want you to leave," he offered.

"Why should that matter to you?"

"Because you're good for Aunt Lucy, she's the happiest I've seen her since Uncle Len died!"

"Coming from you, that's a compliment."

"And we can definitely use more pretty faces on the island," he added.

She stared at him; he knew she was engaged, was there no end to his frivolity?

At her lack of response, Geoff grew serious.

"What can I do to help solve this?"

"I think there is something . . ."

"Just name it!"

"What do you know about Nyls, your Aunt Lucy's help? Where does he come from, did he know my dad . . ."

"Whoa, you don't think Nyls is involved?"

"I don't know what to think. I just feel like he's never liked me and as far as I know I've never done anything to him," she explained.

"Well, Nyls isn't exactly a warm-blooded type," Geoff agreed. "If I had to pick an animal he resembled, I would choose the reptile family."

"Yeah, I know what you mean," Liselle agreed. "He leaves me cold."

"Well, I'll see what I can find out, unobtrusively, of course."

After Geoff left, Liselle replayed their conversation. Wasn't it rather arrogant of him to chop down a tree that wasn't his?

She reached for her artist's pad and did a quick sketch of his features; nice face, good bone structure, sparkling blue eyes; he could turn a girl's head.

On a fresh page she sketched Tom's strong chin, thick dark hair and brooding eyes. Did a person's eyes reflect character or were they simply the result of genes?

Her ideal man had always been tall, dark, and handsome and comparing the two, she realized Tom had worked hard to attain his position in life while Geoff was born with the proverbial silver spoon in his mouth. And Geoff's 'poor little rich boy' attitude did not impress her.

Tom, only a year or two older than Geoff, was light-years ahead of him in experience and maturity. He was a man while Geoff might never attain the same level of maturity. She felt at ease around Geoff for he didn't intimidate her. She didn't care what he thought.

But Tom! Tom had chosen a complex profession and kept her busy anticipating his moods. She would never grow tired of him while Geoff she could see through in a New York minute. He was only out for a good time.

Closing her pad, she glanced up to see Lucy pulling in the driveway, followed by a small pickup. Two men got out and began unloading beds.

"We might as well both be comfortable, Liselle, I brought you a bed."

Liselle rolled her eyes. "You spoil me! Come and sit, I've brewed some tea."

As she recounted Geoff's visit, she abruptly changed the subject.

"Lucy, who helped load the beds?"

"Why, the two workmen, and Nyls got them out of storage."

"Did you tell him why you wanted them?"

"Well, of course, Liselle, I had no reason not to. Why do you ask?"

"I just wondered about Nyls' reaction to you staying here."

"I didn't see any reaction. I just hope the previous vandalism was an isolated event and whoever did it is tired of their little game," Lucy exclaimed.

But you don't really believe that, Liselle thought, or you would let me stay by myself.

18

If the Lord had not been on our side—
the raging waters would have swept us away.

PSALM 124:1,5

THE NEXT MORNING LISELLE rode with Lucy to the mansion and they ate breakfast in the kitchen with Emily before Liselle went in search of Nyls.

"Morning, Nyls," she greeted cheerily.

He met her with a grunt and barely glanced at her.

"What would you like me to do this morning?"

He walked to a stack of pots and turned to face her. "Scrub these."

"Okay, sure."

She got the supplies and began to whistle as she worked.

"Miss Wintersted, I don't appreciate that racket!"

"Excuse me, Nyls. Why don't we get better acquainted then?"

He raised an eyebrow and went back to the potting table.

"What would you like to know about me, Nyls?"

"I s'pect not much!" he retorted.

"Okay, well, tell me about yourself, have you always lived on the island?"

He studied her. "Reckon so," he finally said.

"So, you knew my grandmother McGivens?"

"Yup—near everybody did."

"What was she like, my grandmother?"

"That purty red hair . . ." he stopped and looked at her, his cold eyes boring into her before he turned to spit in a corner.

Shuffling to the tool rack he selected a shovel and returned to the compost pile where he slammed it down.

"Move this compost into the greenhouse," he said and walked out into the misty rain.

Pulling on oversized leather gloves she pushed hard to move the compost before lunch, her muscles aching and mind numb from the monotony, knowing it was probably the last she would see of Nyls today.

Hanging up her shovel, she found Lucy in the kitchen stirring chowder as Emily set the table.

"How's it going, Liselle?"

"Slow . . . I'm going over to the cottage after lunch."

"Do you want me to drive you?"

"Thanks Lucy but I feel like a walk in the rain."

After lunch Liselle tied her hair up under her rain hat, slipped on trench coat and pulled on boots. "I'll see you later," she called as she set out for the cottage. It should be a good afternoon to read by the fire.

Marching past chokeberry and nut orchards she could smell a wood fire; must be a neighbor, she thought, yet found it odd that smoke carried this far.

As she approached, the smell grew stronger and climbing the last hill she could just glimpse her cottage.

A tongue of fire curled from beneath her shed.

"No!" The cry tore from her and racing down the hill, she grabbed a bucket from the porch. Slipping and sliding down the bank, her hat flew off as she lobbed buckets of water at the fire, her efforts in vain as the water sloshed back at her feet before reaching the target.

Her sore muscles screamed from the added exertion as flames began devouring Grant's wreath. The fire would probably catch the cottage, too. Her father's house would be lost.

"God, help me–please help me!" she cried, and sinking down bareheaded on the bank, laying her head on her arms, unwilling to watch the destruction, she cried great rivers that threatened to drown her.

Twilight had fallen when she felt arms lifting her and someone calling her name.

"Liselle, Liselle . . ."

Geoff pulled her up the bank as she realized a torrential rain had come and extinguished the flames. Her cottage was safe.

The shed, however, with two walls and roof already consumed by fire, wobbled on one remaining stilt. With wrenching sound the two remaining walls sandwiched together as weathered boards and rusted nails splintered apart and toppled into the rising creek to be swept away.

Liselle covered her eyes as Geoff pulled her inside the kitchen and tugged off her boots. Wrapping her legs with towels, he threw wood in the Franklin and soon had a pot of tea whistling on the stove.

"Drink this, you need to warm up. I don't know how long you were out there."

"Would your mother approve, Geoff?"

"Of . . . ?"

"Of you helping me?"

"Why wouldn't she?"

"I don't think she ever cared for me."

"My mother is just like that, and I'm old enough to do what I want! Drink your tea." Obediently she complied, the fight having left her. She never believed anyone would harm an old house that had stood deserted for years. Now she believed. Why had she been so stubborn and goaded them to action?

Fresh tears stung her eyes.

It was dark when the headlights of a car flashed across the window and Lucy's face registered shock when she entered.

"My God, what happened?"

"The shed is gone, Lucy."

"Gone, how, Geoff, what . . . ?"

"The shed was on fire! I came along to find Liselle on the bank. The rain put out the fire but the shed was taken by the creek."

"Well, we are not staying here tonight, Liselle, the sooner I get you home the better!"

"This is my home!" she offered weakly.

"Not tonight, finish your tea while Geoff carries your things to the van."

❧

Back in Grandmother's room, Liselle rinsed in a hot shower until the mud was out of her hair, grateful that God had protected her house and responded to her cry for help by sending the rain and Geoff. Otherwise she would probably still be lying in the cold mud.

Slipping into a flannel gown she crawled into the four-poster and reached for Grandmother's journal, turning to an earlier entry.

March 29, 1926

Saddest day of my life, my loss enormous, the reality too brutal to contemplate. I cannot keep my baby, this beautiful child of 9 days that I love more than life. Father has refused to feed another mouth, and Ellen's father has left on a fishing boat. How will I ever survive?

E. Cottington

Liselle's eyes strayed to Grandmother's portrait over the fireplace, once so young and beautiful before life had taken its toll, forced to deal with her loss alone. I have Tom she comforted herself, and Lucy.

Exhausted, Liselle slept soundly that night and dreamt of love: her mother's love, Lucy's, Tom, all floated through her subconscious. At one point she imagined Tom was next to her, stroking her hair. She didn't want to wake up, the dream sweeter than the reality.

Opening her eyes in the pre-dawn light, Tom leaned to kiss her and she wrapped her arms around his neck. "You're here!"

"I drove as fast as I could when Lucy called!"

"Oh, Tom, your trial, she shouldn't have!"

"Hush, I would have been upset if she hadn't."

"I'm glad you came," she breathed and drifted off to sleep.

Quietly he tiptoed down the hall to the kitchen.

"How is she, Tom?" Lucy asked.

"Resting; I can't tell you how much I appreciate your calling."

"You have every right to know, I just hope she doesn't get pneumonia, lying out there like that . . . if Geoff hadn't found her."

"Who?"

"My nephew."

"Well, I owe him my thanks."

The next time Liselle woke, she was sure she had dreamed Tom beside her. Maybe the fire was a nightmare, too, but when she went to the bathroom and saw the mud in the shower, she knew it was real.

Slipping on her robe and pushing damp hair from her face, she shuffled to the kitchen.

"Good morning, gorgeous!"

"Tom!"

"In the flesh . . ."

"You really were here, it wasn't a dream?"

"It was me all right!"

"You were in bed with me . . ." she blushed.

"That's right, and you'd better get used to it if we're getting married. Besides, I have to confess that this time I was a perfect gentleman," he teased.

She kissed him and turned to hug Lucy.

"Lucy, my dear Lucy, what would I do without you? It seems you've been taking care of me since the day we met."

"And what a boring life I would have otherwise," she teased. "Have some breakfast, and we'll talk."

Liselle attacked a stack of pancakes covered with a pitcher of syrup as Emily refilled her orange juice. Lucy gave Tom knowing looks.

"Lucy's right, we have to make some plans and agree to them," Tom began.

"Like what?" Liselle asked.

"You can go over to the cottage and collect your things, or someone can go for you."

"Tom . . ."

"Let me finish. Whatever objection you're going to make, you can't stay there any more, that's obvious."

"I know," she replied meekly, feeling very small. "I was just going to say that I think I made Nyls angry yesterday."

"How did you make him angry?" Tom and Lucy asked together.

"I was trying to get him to talk to me, and he didn't want to, typical Nyls, so I asked him about Grandmother, and that seemed to bother him, he just kind of huffed out. After lunch I walked to the cottage and by the time I got there, the fire had pretty much done its damage."

Fresh tears welled. "I can't believe anyone would really want to burn me out!"

Tom reached to comfort her.

"Try not to think about it. We'll get this figured out. I have an arson investigator going over there today."

"You do!" Liselle was surprised at how fast he worked.

"Yes, and I have information on Nyls that I think you'll find very interesting."

Liselle's attention was diverted by the sound of the doorbell and she turned to see Geoff saunter in.

"Morning Aunt Lucy," he stooped to kiss her cheek.

"Liselle," he turned to her, "I stopped to see how you are?"

"Much better thank you."

"Good, good," he paused. "I also wanted to tell you that I have some information on Nyls if you're up to hearing it?"

"Yes, please," she exclaimed.

Tom scowled at his interruption.

"Well, I asked mother about him, where he came from, and she said he's always been a recluse, lives in a small cabin near the cemetery."

"He lives near my cottage then?" Liselle asked.

"Yes just a few hundred yards away. The cabin is hidden from the road," Geoff explained. "And one more thing, before I forget, it seems that at one time Nyls was sweet on Lizzie Wilson, before she met Hank Wintersted!"

"Wow," Lucy exclaimed. "I didn't know that, so it sounds like he was jilted!"

"Yeah, like a real love triangle or something," Geoff laughed.

"Geoff, you shouldn't joke that way!" Lucy admonished.

"I'm sorry, Aunt Lucy. Well, I better get going. Glad you're better Liselle!"

"Thanks, Geoff, and thanks for rescuing me!" she called as he went out the kitchen door.

"Well, now, if anyone is interested in what my *investigator* found out, I'll be glad to share it!" Tom interjected.

"Oh, Tom, I'm sorry. You were about to tell us something. Please," Liselle apologized.

Mollified, he began, "My investigator did a background check on Nyls Atterley. He has no family on the island, but does have two elderly sisters in Bremerton. Neither he nor they ever married. He enlisted in the Army the year that Hank and Lizzie married, but was sent home a few months later, apparently he washed out. He's lived on the island ever since, doing odd jobs for the locals but mostly employed by the McGivens family."

"I can't believe he knew my father and never said a word," Liselle exclaimed.

"There may be good reason for that," Tom continued. "On checking the area of the fire, my investigator found an Army gas can with the initials "NA" stenciled on the bottom. Dusting for fingerprints he was able to lift a print that matched Nyls Atterley. Checking further, he determined that gasoline was doused on the shed's stilts. That's why it burned so fast. The local authorities have been notified to issue a search warrant for Mr. Atterley's residence. I'm sure they will want to question him."

"I can't believe that Nyls would be involved in anything like this," Lucy defended. "He's always been quiet, did his job and minded his business."

As she tried to fit the pieces together, Liselle kept coming back to the fact that if her father had taken Lizzie away from Nyls, then perhaps Nyls had held a grudge all these years. Once he learned who she was, all those feelings had surfaced and he had reacted out of revenge.

～

Noon came and Nyls didn't show for work. The investigator arrived after searching his cabin, lifting floor boards and checking the crawl space. He handed Tom his report.

A few items were of special interest and Tom gave it to Liselle to read while Lucy looked over her shoulder:

Contents of Nyls Atterley's cabin:

1 nativity set
1 withered tree (apple?-approx. 5 feet in length)
3 cans of black spray paint
1 metal box approx. 12x12 inches contents:
faded blue quilt, 'Grant' embroidered on one edge
2 tortoise shell combs-initials "LW" carved
newspaper articles

Liselle opened the metal box and fingered the ragged blue quilt, still soft after all these years. It was obvious that Nyls had taken the nativity set from her porch, as well as the apple tree that Geoff had jokingly chopped down. The black spray paint certainly looked suspicious enough; with proof of his theft and the right questions, he would soon confess.

She scanned the newspaper clippings: Hank's and Lizzie's wedding announcement, the twins' birth announcement, the drowning; an occasional mention of Grandmother McGivens, and finally, Lizzie's obituary.

She placed everything back in the box and looked up at Tom.

"What will happen to Nyls?"

"When the authorities find him, he will have to face criminal charges, with some rather serious consequences."

"I feel sorry for him," she said, "loving Lizzie all this time and never getting over her choosing my father. It's too bad he never got on with his life and had a family of his own."

"Speaking of which," Tom said, "how about us getting on with our lives?"

"What about Nyls?" she asked.

"He will turn up somewhere; he's certainly not going to bother you. If he is in hiding, it won't be on this island. It's mostly circumstantial evidence but with the theft, Nyls should confess and plea bargain any jail time."

He touched her arm and she gazed into his glowing eyes.

"I mean it Liselle, you can stop worrying about him. I want us to pick a date."

She clutched her still damp hair.

"Oh, no, I'm a frightful mess. I need to change and freshen up!"

"No more delays, I want to marry you rumpled nightgown, wet hair, and all," he stated.

"Really?" she said.

"Really," he repeated. "Lucy, where's your calendar?"

As Lucy went to get her planner, Liselle walked to the kitchen window and gazed out at the willow tree that shaded the duck pond. Getting on with your life, that's what it was all about, not allowing setbacks or disappointments to stop you. Now was the time to plan their future.

"Here we are," Lucy said, entering the room.

They were married in Lucy's back yard on a warm sunny day in mid-April the first spring after Ellen's death as crocuses, tulips and daffodils pushed through the earth.

Standing before the judge under the willow tree with Lucy and Geoff as their witnesses, Liselle wore a tailored suit of winter white with an emerald silk blouse and carried her mother's Bible with a single white rose on top.

Lucy's wedding gift of "something old" was Grandmother's antique emerald earrings that Liselle wore for her only jewelry.

After a catered lunch, they were off to the ferry, Tom having told Liselle to pack for beach weather but not even Lucy knew their honeymoon destination.

On the ferry they snuggled in the car and once on land, his adrenalin soaring, Tom pushed the car into high gear and raced for the airport, alone at last with his bride.

"Tom, you have to tell me where we're going before we get to the gate," she teased and happy to placate her, he relented.

"There's this little island called Sint Maarten in the Caribbean . . ."

"It sounds Dutch."

"Yes and French, you're going to love it. The water is turquoise, like nothing you've ever seen. We can be as lazy as we want, lie around and get tanned, snorkel, catamaran to the other islands; forget about the world for a week."

It sounded perfect. They had met and married on Anderson Island, their marriage would begin on Sint Maarten and soon she would visit St. Paul, the island of his birth.

She felt such peace as she gazed into her husband's glowing eyes, her heart committed to this handsome man. Whatever it took, she would make their marriage everything he desired; visiting Alaska, meeting his family all part of their future.

Her mother's death the catalyst for her journey toward life and love, Ellen's last words echoed in her mind: "Liselle, don't be afraid to live your life!"

Had her grandparents not shared the secret of her mother's adoption, she would never have found Lucy, or Tom. Her heart filled with joy as she recalled a favorite Bible verse:

Those who hope in the Lord will renew their strength, they will soar on wings like eagles, they will run and not grow weary, they will walk and not faint. Isa 40:31

God was her strength. With such a *heavenly* father, who was she, the created, to argue with the Creator: "Why did you let this happen?"

Thank you, Lord, she breathed, for teaching me to wait.

Part 2

The Sweet Years

19

ANOTHER EVENING ALONE AS Liselle clicked through the TV channels and recalled Tom's earlier phone call. "Don't wait up, I'll be late," he had said and a pang of fear shot through her.

She hated having to tell the girls again, another day of not seeing their father. He left before they woke each morning and with frequent late night clients, his presence was rare in their little worlds.

It was probably just her pregnancy hormones causing these feelings of doubt and insecurity for Tom had given her no reason to question his absence. Still, she couldn't deny the sense of unease that crept in and resting her hand on her expanding waist she felt the baby kick. She loved her husband; the man she never thought she would have, charismatic and intelligent, interesting, energetic, with a deep sense of right and wrong.

During their whirl-wind courtship she hadn't stopped to consider what obstacles they might face or the differences between them, choosing to believe they could talk out any conflicts. Usually though, Tom was just too tired to talk or he simply wasn't there. Had she married in haste?

Looking back, she was glad they had two years of married life before the twins came, living in her mother's bungalow while hunting for the perfect property to build their dream house.

From the beginning Tom had delegated the care of the home to her, depending on her to keep him organized while he plunged ahead in his career. Gladly she had accepted the challenge of pleasing her young energetic husband, of meeting his expectations. And he had many expectations.

She thought about her expectations and how they had yet to materialize. He did not share her love of God, nor did he seem to enjoy church activities. Each morning she prayed that he would see the importance of God in their marriage.

Sweet, attentive, a passionate lover he worked long hours while she devoted her time to fulfilling the social demands as wife of a young and successful attorney. She chuckled to think how much she had become like Lucy, attending luncheons, fund raisers, and charities with other wives. It had opened a whole new world to her.

And when Tom had taken her to Alaska that first summer to meet his family, it was then she became painfully aware of the divide between them. It was bittersweet now to recall that first awkward meeting.

Looking back on that beautiful spring day when they had just returned from their wedding trip to the Caribbean, she was grilling steaks on the patio when she heard a car pull in the driveway.

It didn't sound like Tom's car and going to investigate, she nearly collided with him.

"Tom, whose car is?"

"Ours . . ."

"It's a Jaguar."

"Right, remember that big trial I just finished, well this firm really knows how to show its appreciation. Come on, I'll take you for a spin!"

"But dinner's ready."

"Just a quick trip around the block," he begged.

"The steaks will be ruined," she argued.

"We'll go out to dinner," he countered and once again surprised by his cavalier approach to money, knowing he wouldn't give up until she said yes, she had relented and put the steaks away for another meal.

On the drive south and into the surrounding hillside Tom had raced the car over newly paved roads with breathtaking views of Mount Rainier, his speed making her nervous.

"Tom, slow down!"

He hit the brakes and backed up grinning, to stop at newly cleared land. She caught her breath at the view. "You already knew about this," she accused.

"Yes," he admitted. "The land has just listed. We have our choice of any lot."

≈

Over dinner at a tiny Italian restaurant he had another surprise, "My secretary has booked our trip to Alaska next month."

She stared at him wondering how he could plan such a trip without consulting her. Did he not think she might have plans? Of course she didn't, but still she had assumed they would plan it together instead of him telling her to pack and be ready.

"You will love it and my parents want to meet you," he continued.

"When do we leave?"

"In two weeks; pack your coat, it will be chilly," he explained. "And just to make it more pleasant, I bought you this."

She took the long gold box and slipped off the purple bow. From the folds of tissue paper, she lifted black cashmere, the black fur collar brushing her cheek. "It's beautiful!"

Tom smiled. "You'll look beautiful, and you'll appreciate it in Alaska. We'll take the coaster train to Bremerton, fly to Anchorage and then Dutch Harbor where my brothers will meet and ferry us to St. Paul."

"It sounds complicated and remote. What else should I know about this island," she teased.

"I should probably mention that there's no bank," he laughed. "And no shopping!"

～

So began married life, Tom always in motion, her schedule unpredictable as he decided everything without consulting her. She was surprised at how easy it had been to let him take over.

Before she knew it, two weeks had passed and they were landing at the tiny air strip on Dutch Harbor. While Tom waited for his brothers she ducked across the street to the Cathedral of the Holy Ascension, its golden domes and carved icons reminding her of places she had once visited with mother.

Soon Tom was calling her and she raced down the steps, almost colliding with three men standing beside him. Tom frowned at her.

"Henry, Nathan and Ivan," he introduced. Henry was older than Tom, the twins Nathan and Ivan younger. She was surprised that all three had fair skin, blond hair and blue eyes. Only Tom it seemed had inherited the dark good looks of the native Aleutian.

Collecting their luggage and stowing it aboard the ferry, Ivan stood by Liselle smiling as the ferry pulled away from the dock. "Welcome, Liselle."

"Thank you," she instantly warmed to him, intrigued with his accent.

"I hope you like our family," he said.

"I'm sure I will. What do you do out here?"

"Oh, many things; hunt seal, tuna, we work all the time." He threw his arms open in an expansive gesture. She smiled and looked over to see Tom frowning again.

"And how are your parents, Ivan?"

"They are well. They live in the old way," he explained.

"The old way?" she asked.

"In barabaras."

"Oh, I see," she said, but didn't.

"Ivan," shouted Henry, "tend to the lines starboard!"

Tom came to drape a heavy skin over her shoulders.

"We have a long ride across the Bering Sea, but it's a good day for travel," he explained.

The hide was dusty and heavy, but surprisingly warm. "What animal . . ." she asked.

"Reindeer," Tom replied. "They have a third lung to keep them warm. The villagers eat every part."

"You're serious?" she asked

"Yes, absolutely; even the ears and lips!"

She shuddered and thought better of saying "yuck". Tom was so matter of fact and she realized how very little she knew about the land of his childhood.

"And what about the caribou, your family name . . . ?"

"Caribou means "life" once our main diet. In winter the villagers ate the contents of the stomach for the vitamins in the grasses to ward off scurvy, you know, the lack of Vitamin C," he explained.

With the wind at her back, Liselle pulled her hood over her head and faced north to watch for the island as the ferry chugged through calm glacial waters. It was a strange, beautiful land, reminding of Washington yet with its own unique charm.

Dusk had fallen as they approached from the south, the area's balmy 50 degrees having dipped lower. As the ferry chugged around the island's hook shape to a small inlet on the leeward side, Liselle studied the low barren hills.

A low fog had moved in and she was glad she had thought to wear long johns under her jeans. She shivered as they docked at the deserted beach.

"*It will be chilly*," Tom had said. "Chilly" would have been nice. This was cold.

"Where are the people," she asked.

"Having their evening meal," Tom answered, taking her arm. "I know it looks barren but wildlife is abundant here."

They crunched across the stony beach, Liselle straining to see in the distance where smoke rose. Climbing a steep incline, the men stopped on a grassy knoll next to a large mound of earth.

"Here we are," Tom announced and she looked at him as though he had sprouted horns. Then she saw the small ladder next to the portal in the roof. Realizing they waited for her, she climbed up and down the ladders and was immediately surrounded by children and women all chattering in another language.

Turning back to the ladder, an enormous woman blocked her way, the braids on her head making her appear taller. Silently she appraised Liselle.

"This way dotch-ka," she took Liselle's arm.

"My name is Liselle," she began.

"Um, dotch-ka mean daughter . . . Tom pick skinny one," she confirmed squeezing Liselle's arm. "Mama," she pointed to herself and led Liselle to a pile of furs at her fireside; motioned her to sit and scattered the children trying to touch her hair.

"Thank you," Liselle said as Tom arrived.

"I see you've met my mother," he said.

"Kak, Tomas?"

"Mama, please speak English."

"Kak? Um . . . how you marry skinny girl? She not give babies!"

"That's our business, mama," he explained.

"Oh, mama not know, you big law-man, now mama not know?"

He went to stand beside her. "Mama," he whispered, "Please don't make Liselle feel bad, that's all I meant okay?"

"Govaresch pa-russki, Tomas!"

"I will not speak Russian with Liselle here," he countered.

Mama ignored him and turned to the cooking pots. "I make Piroshki, you hungry?"

"I would love to try some," Liselle replied, and carefully chewed the seal pastry.

"And where is Papa?" Tom asked.

"Oh, he will come," Ivan explained.

Liselle noticed a dark haired beauty next to Henry. Dressed in soft tunic and leggings with black hair that flowed down the curve of her back and spilled over her obviously pregnant front, at Liselle's glance, Henry introduced his wife, Nedelia.

A racket ensued near the entrance and Henry announced, "That will be papa." He glanced at Nedelia and she rose to serve her father-in-law. Something in their silent exchange bothered Liselle, but she had no time to ponder with the arrival of her father-in-law. Dressed in an ornamented kamleika, he slipped the robe from his shoulders and carefully removed a carved wooden visor decorated with sea lion whiskers as Ivan let out a muffled laugh.

"Why you laugh," Papa responded and Ivan rolled on his side laughing louder. "Papa, Liselle is already afraid of us. You didn't have to dress up," he explained as everyone joined in laughter.

"I think Liselle has had enough for today," Tom said pulling her to her feet. "We're going to bed."

He led her to the far corner of the area where sleeping compartments were separated by grass mats ringing the large central room. Here he had rigged canvas and pointed to the furs where they would sleep.

With eyes as big as saucers, she undressed down to her long-johns and slipped beneath the skins. Eagerly he joined her.

"I've always wanted to make love in my parents' dwelling," he began.

"Don't even think about it," she replied through clenched teeth and turning her back to him, she huddled under the furs.

"I could shun you for refusing me," he stated.

The trip, the food, the language barrier, and now the primitive bed, had all taken their toll and she was at her limit. "What are you, a cave man?" she responded. "Don't even speak to me."

Liselle slept poorly that night and woke several times to hear rustling in the sod structure above her head supported by whale bones. The dwelling was snug, the seal oil they burned in their lamps stinky; a headache plagued her.

Again the pastry for breakfast along with dried fish; she sat near the entrance hoping for fresh air as she nibbled a crust of bread. What had she gotten herself into? Did Tom really think she would enjoy this?

Just then Tom took her hand. "Let's go for a walk."

It was chilly and she snuggled into the fur of her cashmere, appreciating its warmth. As they walked around the village she marveled at the tiny flowers poking through the barren ground as speckled ptarmigan scurried away. She recalled reading that the islands attracted bird watchers and was home to many species not found in the rest of North America.

Near the water's edge the men repaired angyaqs, large skin boats, while the women pounded more skins. Nedelia worked beside them and curious, Liselle asked, "Did Henry and Nedelia date long?"

"No, that's not how it's done. In the old days there was a bride price. Originally I was to marry Nedelia and Henry was engaged to another. When his intended left the island and I told them I was marrying you, it was decided Henry would marry Nedelia."

Carefully Tom edited how much to tell Liselle, for he realized, seeing Nedelia again, that she would always have a place in his heart.

"So the family was upset that you didn't marry Nedelia?"

"Oh, yeah," Tom replied. "You could say that but I married you because I wanted to; that's just the way it is. I'm sorry for last night, I wasn't being very sensitive."

"You told me almost nothing of what to expect. I guess I'm not handling the trip very well," she explained.

"You're a real trooper," he assured. "But enough for this first time; we'll stay one more night since the ferry doesn't run today. Tomorrow we'll go to Sitka and home."

At her sigh of relief, Tom began to chuckle.

"What's so funny?" she asked.

"Red hair," he said. "I bet they'll be talking about you for years!"

"Why?" she was smiling with him.

"The explorer Shelikhov came to these shores from Russia, maybe 200 years ago. His wife was the first white woman and she's still talked about. I imagine our visit has been quite the event," he explained.

That evening Liselle chewed more bread crusts; missing her fresh fruit and vegetables, though Tom reminded her of the foliage in the animals' stomachs.

"Thank you very much," she replied, "I'll wait until home."

He laughed out loud. "Here's another fact for you, my sweet little repository of information," he said. At her interested look, he continued, "You saw the little speckled ptarmigan today? In August they turn white to camouflage for winter."

"Well, Mr. Caribou, if you're trying to impress me, you're certainly succeeding," she bantered. "But one thing I've always wondered?"

"What's that," he asked.

"The northern lights, what are they like, since I'm never going to see them?"

"Oh, you really must see them once," he teased.

"No way, you'll have to tell me about them," she protested.

"Would it impress you to know that the atmosphere gets a semi-violet haze, the snow so crisp it crackles?"

"Really!" she exclaimed.

"The aurora borealis is really something," he vowed.

The next day, Liselle's antenna was up and she found herself watching Nedelia. Although Tom never spoke to her or looked at her, Liselle was plagued with feelings of insecurity. She was beautiful and of his world; there had been an understanding between them.

She sensed tension in Henry, as well, shouting at Nedelia over the smallest things—his soup too cool, his tea too hot; Liselle fought the urge to tell him to set it outside for a second.

Mama seemed oblivious to everything and everyone except Tom, becoming distant when they started packing. Unhappy that the visit was short, she began heaping guilt on him.

"Tomas, we no give permission to stay away!" Mama reprimanded and slipping into Russian she continued to scold. Liselle had not warmed to his mother, though she tried. They were worlds apart and might never be close.

As far as she was concerned, their visits would be few and far between, this one merely a courtesy visit. Now she and Tom were free to resume their lives in Olympia.

She did wonder how mama would manage if she visited them and on the ferry to Dutch Harbor, she asked Tom. "Has your mother ever left St. Paul?"

"I'm not sure," he replied. "If she did, it was many years ago. Why?"

"Well, I was wondering if she would ever visit us."

"You mean in Olympia?"

"Well, yes," she explained.

"Never happen," he replied, "in a thousand years, never, ever happen."

Liselle wondered if that was Tom's preference or his mother's.

In Sitka, they toured St. Michael's Cathedral, a prominent landmark on the city's skyline, reminding that it was once the capital of Russian America.

"The parish priest moved here a few years ago," Tom offered. "If we come in autumn there are maybe a hundred whales feeding in the harbor before they trek to Hawaii," he explained.

"You mean the whales go to Hawaii for the winter?"

"That's right," he smiled. "Even they won't stay if they don't have to."

"Someday maybe we could visit St. Lazaria and the volcanic cliffs," Liselle added.

"Sure," he agreed, "Although with my case load I don't know when that would be."

At this news, she breathed a sigh of relief, thankful for once that he had a heavy schedule. They flew to Seattle and rented a car to Olympia, unwilling to wait for the slower coaster train.

20

AFTER THAT FIRST BUMPY encounter, the next two years passed quickly as Liselle met with the architect, builder, and interior designer, Tom giving her free rein to plan their future home. Lucy helped decorate and with her sure sense of style each room became what Liselle had envisioned.

One room in particular Liselle gave extra attention to: the nursery and hoped her mother-in-law's prediction wrong about her ability to reproduce for Nedelia had given birth twice.

Tom didn't seem concerned but when Liselle discovered she was pregnant and the sonogram revealed twins, he was over the moon. She marveled as well, though they shouldn't have been surprised, her father had twin sons and Tom had twin brothers.

Shortly after the twins were born, Tom became a partner at Synder, Evans & Wells; his bonuses, salary and workload in keeping with his new status. By then he had put away all memories of a poverty-filled childhood, determined that his wife and children would never know such.

Liselle had no objection to Tom's family visiting them, but was adamant that the children not go to the Pribilof Islands, not while they were young. There was plenty of time when they were older.

Claire and Chloe were eight months when Tom came home with news that his parents were coming to visit.

"Tom, you were so sure they would nev-er come," Liselle admonished.

"My parents want to check out the university for Ivan. Don't worry, it's only a couple of days and I will try to get home early," he promised.

"You're not serious about leaving me alone with them? I barely know them! We haven't seen them in . . . three years!"

"You will be fine, I know you can do it," he replied.

"No, I can't! I don't know them. You'll have to take off," she responded.

"I can't take off, I'm busy."

"Tom, you will be here, or I won't be!"

"What's that supposed to mean?"

"I will go to Lucy's, so you just decide how to get the time off," she stated. She hated to argue, but her discomfort around his family outweighed reason. She didn't want to entertain his family alone, nor was it fair with the language barrier and their unfamiliarity with modern living.

∽

On the day of their arrival, Tom left early with a promise to return at noon. Mid-morning, as Liselle finished cleaning, the doorbell rang. They were early and she'd had no time to relax or change clothes. She was relieved to see Ivan, remembering his friendliness in Alaska.

Tom called as they were getting settled. "I'm really sorry. I can't get away for another couple of hours."

"I'm in the middle of fixing lunch and the girls are just up from their naps."

"I'm really sorry . . ."

She hung up on him. Somehow she had known this would happen. She would just have to make the best of it. Too bad she hadn't thought to invite Lucy.

It was at times like this that she really missed her mother.

∽

Tom's mother tried to coax the toddlers to come to her but they would have none of it, Chloe crawling to Liselle and clinging to her jeans while Claire sat in the corner and screamed. Finally Mama pulled a matroishka from her bag and began to pull apart the tiny stacking dolls. With the girls occupied, Liselle finished putting lunch on the table.

Afterwards, Liselle showed them the house, mama commenting on the size, color, and cost. While her in-laws rested in the guest room, Liselle had coffee in the kitchen with Ivan as the girls played on the floor nearby.

"Thanks for your help, Ivan, the girls really seemed to warm to you," she said.

"They are great kids, one looks like you and one like Tom," he replied.

"Yes, they are a special part of our lives," she agreed. "How did your parents handle the trip?"

"Not too bad," he said and started to chuckle.

"What?" she asked.

"Mama had everyone scurrying out of her way at the airport, she moves very fast for a big woman. Papa and I had to run to keep up with her," he smiled at the memory. "I'm afraid we were quite unorthodox! Hah, listen to me, unorthodox! We grew up orthodox."

Liselle joined in his hearty laughter and didn't hear Tom come in.

"What's so funny?" Tom said.

"We didn't hear you come in," she explained to Tom.

"What were you laughing at," he pursued.

"Oh, just a play on words . . ."

Stung over his failure to be home as promised, he could just wonder what he had missed. After all, he kept her in the dark about a great deal of his day; not to mention his family.

"Well, I'm home for the evening," he offered.

"Why don't you and Ivan take the girls in the den while I clean up lunch," she offered. She had just taken a tray of iced tea into the den and settled down in the window seat when her in-laws joined them. Hurrying to get their beverages, she realized it was time to set the dinner table.

"Me cook," mama offered from the lounger.

"Oh, I have everything planned. Dessert is ready, there's a roast in the oven and potatoes. I just need to fix the salad. Why don't you relax?"

At Mama's wide-eyed look, Liselle realized she had spoken too fast and slowly she began again, "Thank you, but I have dinner started."

"I make bortsch for you and Tomas," Mama insisted, getting out of the recliner.

"Mama," Tom interrupted, "We don't have the ingredients for that."

"Then you go get 'greedy ants,'" she commanded.

Liselle looked from Tom to his mother and back to Tom. "Okay," he said.

"What? O-kay?" she said, following him to the kitchen. "I have the meal planned and I don't want bortsch!"

"It will make her happy and keep her busy."

"I'm putting my foot down. I ate their food; they can eat ours."

"I know," he agreed. "But we're going to have all kinds of problems if mama doesn't make bortsch."

"You're going to have all kinds of problems if mama does make bortsch." They stared at each other, not budging until Tom picked up his car keys and headed for the garage.

At Chloe's scream, Liselle dashed for the den where Claire whined and grabbed her leg. Swinging a toddler to each shoulder, she walked down the hall to the bathroom and closed the door.

Unable to hold back the tears, she sat the girls on the counter and pulled tissue from the roller, wiping her eyes and nose as two pairs of eyes watched. When she returned to the kitchen, Ivan took the girls and she began to fix the salad. She smiled at him through misty eyes.

"It's not my business . . ." he began.

"It's alright, Ivan. I apologize for carrying on like this."

"Are you happy . . ." he asked.

"Happy . . . ? We have a good life, Tom just seems different when he's around his family, his mother," she explained.

"Tom has always been different," Ivan said.

"How is he different?"

"At the mission school, always curious about the outside world while the rest of us were content on the island. Tom wanted to explore, his favorite book the world atlas. Now I think he just wants to make up for breaking Mama's heart."

"How did he break . . . ?" she asked.

"By not marrying . . ." Ivan stopped. His face flushed and he shifted the girls, locking his attention on them and their fascination with his bone necklace.

". . . Nedelia," she finished for him. "And what about you, will you marry?"

"My wife is already picked. But I won't marry for another couple of years. Our parents have consented to me attending the University. It took a long time with Tomas staying away but finally they said yes. Besides, I want to pursue a medical degree."

"Really," Liselle was impressed.

"Yes, you know the women of my village excel in natural doctoring. I learned at my mother's side and am now in love with medicine."

"And will you leave the island?"

"No, we need medical people; my heart and my home will always be there," he explained.

"And how does your fiancée feel about waiting to marry?"

"Oh, well," he grinned. "You know the hot Aleutian blood. We don't stay away from each other."

Embarrassed at his youthful revelation, Liselle finished preparing the salad in silence.

~

Tom returned with the groceries. "Here they are," he said, smiling. She eyed him coolly.

"Are you helping make bortsch?" he asked.

"When pigs fly," she answered and gathering the girls from Ivan, she walked to the den where his parents sat engrossed in TV.

"Now just a minute," he hurried after her and caught her shoulder. She turned to face him.

"Mama can show you," he instructed.

"You can kiss my foot!"

Her face was hot, her eyes stormy as she turned to go up the stairs.

"Where are you going?"

"To put the girls down for their nap; are you gone so much that you don't even know their schedule?"

Her retort stung and he followed her into the nursery.

"I want to speak with you in our room," he said in a low controlled voice.

She obeyed and stood just inside their bedroom door.

"Why can't you be nice?" he asked.

"You know what, I'm really very tired, and you don't have a clue, do you?"

"Oh sure, like you did anything today," he attacked. "Why don't you try going to the office? Then you'd know what tired is!"

At her stunned expression, he slammed out, her tears falling hotter and faster at his low blow. Couldn't he see how hard she was trying? She stayed in their bathroom trying to control her emotions. When she finally came downstairs, she heard muffled conversation in the kitchen where Tom sat while mama chopped beets.

In one day her whole world seemed to implode. Why was Tom acting so mean, like he didn't care about her or the girls? If their marriage was over, where would she go, to Lucy's? Her head hurt as the questions buzzed around.

Mealtime was tense as everyone ate two separate meals prepared by the women, the men casting furtive looks, no one pretending that everything was fine. The girls slept through dinner and were cranky when they woke refusing to eat. Liselle gave them teething cookies while she did the dishes, her in-laws in the den enthralled with the television.

Tom took Ivan out for a beer and when they returned, Liselle had gone to bed with Claire and Chloe snuggled on each side of her. Tom slept in the den that night.

His family left the next day, but not before the rift between Tom and Liselle widened. She resented his going to the office before sunrise, leaving her to deal with mama's sullen mood, papa's stolen glances and Ivan's vain attempts to make her smile.

If Tom had ever expressed a desire for her to cook his native dishes, she would have learned. It was then she realized their problems were deeper than a pot of bortsch.

2 1

Drink water from your own cistern,
running water from your own well.

PROV 5:15

PUTTING HER MEMORIES ASIDE, she rose awkwardly and climbed the stairs to the playroom. Situated on the south side of the house between the nursery and the master bedroom, it was a cheerful room in shades of yellow and apricot, ruffled curtains at the windows.

Here she had hung the canvas that she started the week she had met Lucy. Now it caught her eye, the reds and blacks joined by daffodil yellow and robin's egg blue. An abstract certainly and not her favorite style, but it seemed to capture her journey from the darks of that time to light, from sadness to joy.

Standing in the doorway she gazed at the girls, loved to watch them, Claire with the fiery red hair, blue eyes and temperamental ways; Chloe with dark eyes and hair, the quick impish smile.

They had turned three last week; so much they had learned, so much yet to teach. And she would teach them. Tom was an excellent father but they knew how to dazzle him. Discipline usually fell to her.

Tom's parents had not visited in the two years since, nor had he mentioned visiting Alaska and after those first bumpy years, their lives had settled into a comfortable routine. They both loved to entertain and life flowed in a dependable pattern.

She still didn't like Tom's schedule but willed herself to accept it. Perhaps in a few years, family time would be normal.

It had drizzled all afternoon and she was bored. On sudden inspiration, she decided to call Lucy. Lucy had slowed down in the last few years, didn't visit as much but welcomed every opportunity to see them. Tom, however, seemed increasingly unable to visit the island.

"Lucy!"

"What's up?"

"If you don't mind a late dinner, I want to drive up with the girls and spend the weekend."

"Do you think you should travel?"

"I'm fine and I miss you!"

"Well, I'm a little concerned about you traveling with the girls and all . . . of course I'd love to have you come."

"The girls will snack and probably sleep. If it won't spoil your plans . . ."

"Not at all, just remember the last ferry leaves at 7:00."

Hanging up the phone, Liselle checked Tom's dress shirts that the cleaners had dropped off an hour ago and laid out a fresh suit so he could dress quickly in the morning, or whenever he got home. Packing clothes and the girls' favorite toys, she left a note for Tom on the bathroom mirror.

With the girls bundled in sweats, she strapped them in the Jeep with their favorite blankets and backing out of the garage, punched the opener and the door creaked down.

She was just ahead of rush hour and traffic was light. Rain drizzled all the way to Kent as she hit every light green.

Weaving her way to Steilacoom, the ferry was loading when she arrived and parked where the attendant directed her. The girls had slept the entire trip; she hoped they would last another twenty minutes.

Leaning her head against the seat rest she closed her eyes. Ah, romance, whatever happened to it? Would Tom even notice she was gone, slipping in and trying not to wake her, very considerate of her pregnancy which had come as a pleasant surprise to them. He would probably find her note in the morning.

∼

Lucy's face was wreathed in smiles as Liselle pulled into the driveway and parked near the carriage house. Exiting the back seat with Claire in her arms, Lucy gathered Chloe and they entered the kitchen.

Emily, Lucy's cook of many years, had died the year before and now the girls devoured the meal Lucy had prepared as if they hadn't seen food in weeks.

"I've missed the island, thanks for letting us come."

"How could I say no to my favorite cousin?"

"Your only cousin . . ." They laughed, Liselle always happiest around Lucy, missing the time they had spent together before she married.

"How are you feeling?"

"Oh, fine! The doctor says everything is fine. It should be a routine birth."

"And how is Tom?"

"Tom is Tom. He works hard; he works all the time, the girls and I rarely see him. Of course I knew his profession was like this, sort of, I guess, but I had hoped it would be different, that somehow he would find time for us."

"He loves you and the children."

"Yes, of course," Liselle agreed, but she didn't feel convinced. His fast-paced career, his need to conquer the world seemed to take him in the opposite direction of her slower-paced motherly duties. Perhaps if family lived closer things would be different, the time spent together creating warm memories and stronger ties.

Lucy was not that far away yet Tom seemed resistant to visit. Liselle wondered if he regretted marrying. She didn't want to raise the children alone, yet felt like she was.

As Lucy tucked the girls in bed in the room next to hers, Liselle snuggled into Grandmother's comfy four-poster, feeling quite matronly with her long hair spread across her flannel gown and the baby gently kicking. Here she always felt comfortable and safe, but safe from what?

"*Tell him,*" the Voice echoed in the deepest part of her being.

"What, Lord?" Liselle responded.

Again the Voice resonated, "*Tell Tom about your love for me.*"

"Yes, of course," she agreed. She recognized the still small Voice after all these years of listening, following, praying. It made perfect sense to include the Lord in their marriage, but Tom wasn't ready to hear. She fell asleep exhausted.

∼

Tom crept into his dark house, leaving the Jaguar in the driveway to avoid the noisy garage door. He heard the den clock strike 4:00 as he slipped down the hall and felt his way through the bedroom, dropping his clothes in a heap and easing into their California king. Liselle rarely stirred these days when he came to bed, exhausted from pregnancy and caring for the girls. Tonight he was glad she was a sound sleeper.

He had never been this late before. Working with the new law intern one thing had led to another. He would definitely reassign Kristyn, her demands on his time now out of control. He hoped she didn't plan to work tomorrow. He would sleep in, breakfast with Liselle and the girls, put in 6–8 hours at the office and swing by the Club before heading home.

Liselle didn't drink, not even a glass of wine and was unaware of his daily trips to the Club for lunch and a martini, another on his way home each evening, charging the bill to the firm's generous expense account.

≈

He slept later than planned and sunlight streaming through the window woke him. He sat up with a start and brushed his tousled hair aside to gaze at his wife's empty side of the bed that was already made. She must be fixing his breakfast.

He stumbled to the bathroom to find her note taped to the mirror:

"Darling, the girls and I have gone to the island for the weekend—back Sunday for dinner—wish you would join us!"

What in the world? What was she thinking, going off on her own like that, pregnant and with two kids? A sense of unease crept over him. Was he missing something?

He would definitely be home for dinner tomorrow when she returned, the billable hours could wait. And he would talk to her! She could be headstrong, but this was too much.

He dressed quickly in the clothes she had laid out and raced his Jaguar to the Club for a late brunch before heading to the office.

As he and his associate Alec began compiling their case research into the various legal documents, he felt excitement as the pleadings took shape. This was when he loved his profession: theory and research coming together to generate positive outcomes in the lives of others. And it didn't hurt that the monetary rewards were substantial.

Pleased with their progress, they quit early to hit the Club. "Come on, Alec, I'll give you a ride over and bring you back to your car," Tom offered.

"That's okay, Tom, I'll take my car. Then if you want to stay longer, I have wheels."

"Why would I want to stay longer?" Tom asked.

Alec shrugged.

"Okay, see you there," Tom agreed and raced through rainy deserted streets. He loved this car; it was made to move. Arriving several minutes before Alec, he was finishing his martini when he spotted Alec and almost choked on his olive. The pretty blond beside him was Kristyn!

I should leave, he thought, before she sees me. Too late, her face lit up in a smile and she sauntered over with Alec in tow.

"Hello, stranger!" she greeted. To Alec she added, "Look who we found!"

"Hello, Kristyn."

"How's the project going?" she continued.

"It's going great, actually," Tom replied, "We got a lot accomplished, thanks to all your research yesterday."

"Yes," she teased, "I would say the research was quite successful."

She left Alec's side to sit beside Tom and taking his arm, brushed a kiss on his cheek. He made no attempt to dissuade her and Alec cleared his throat as he looked away.

"Uh, look, you two, I just remembered someone I need to see." Alec made a hasty retreat.

"Well," Tom began, "did you have dinner yet?"

"No, I didn't," Kristyn replied, "and yes I'd love to!"

Motioning to the waiter to bring a menu, he would get her dinner and give her new work assignments; then go home.

On his second cocktail, he relaxed as Kristyn chatted about different projects she had researched at other law firms. Occasionally she touched his hand and rubbed her knee against his thigh.

By his third cocktail he had forgotten the subject of her reassignment.

After dinner they lingered over cordials as he tried to think of a way to extend the evening. He didn't like going home to an empty house and Kristyn was young, attentive, attractive, and available. She made their relationship easy and her intensity excited him. Besides, the world hadn't ended when he and Nedelia were intimate; who was he hurting by being friendly? And the Bible said you were supposed to love each other.

"Why don't you drive me home," she purred, "I have some books on famous lawyers!"

"Okay, I'm putty in your hands," he smiled into her sparkling green eyes, doubting they would ever open a book, but it certainly sounded harmless.

22

Saturday morning Liselle slept until 8:00 which since the twins' birth felt like sleeping in. Lucy had the girls in the kitchen when Liselle entered, and was relieved to see the pale shadows under Liselle's eyes had faded. She looked brighter this morning and more relaxed.

"Good morning!" they both exclaimed.

"Mommy, mommy!" the twins added in stereo.

"Yes, darlings, look what Auntie made for you, smiley face pancakes." The girls giggled as she poured the syrup. "Mommy, what are we doing today?"

"Well, we can visit the duck pond out back . . ."

"The duck pond, the duck pond," the girls clamored.

After breakfast, clutching crusts of bread they raced on tiny legs to feed the ducks as Liselle smiled to think that in her third trimester, she now moved at the same pace as Lucy.

Afterwards, Liselle drove to the tiny cottage that Tom refused to stay in. Leaving the girls in the car with Lucy, she unlocked the front door and stepped inside where peace filled the dim rooms that she loved.

She walked to the kitchen and gazed out at the spot where the shed once stood. Returning to the car, she announced her decision to Lucy.

"I'm staying here tonight with the girls, you won't be upset?"

Lucy gazed into her eyes. "No, of course not; is there something you want to tell me?"

Liselle turned away as tears filled her eyes. "I just have this desire to be in my father's house, in the place he loved."

"You can talk to me."

"Yes I know."

"Everything is the way you left it," Lucy explained. "We can get extra blankets from my house."

"Thanks Lucy. We'll be over tomorrow after church and have lunch before we start back."

~

After she took Lucy home, Liselle drove to the cottage, settled the girls in the back bedroom for quiet time and curled up with a book by the Franklin stove.

In early afternoon, they walked to a sunny spot where one lonely stilt pushed up from the bank, a silent witness to what had been.

Claire ran to the stilt that came to her waist and tugged at it. "Mommy, what is it?"

Chloe looked up from the berries she was gathering.

"Chloe, don't eat the berries," Liselle admonished.

Kneeling beside Claire, Liselle stroked her silky red hair and explained how a little shed used to be there but washed away in a storm.

Claire laughed at the shed's demise as Chloe joined her to examine the post before turning sad eyes to her mother.

"Why don't we put it back?" she inquired.

"Well, Chloe," Liselle placed her arms around both of them, "sweetheart, we don't really need a shed."

"But something should be here," Chloe continued to worry.

Claire chimed in, "Yes, mommy, something should be here."

Liselle studied the silent eyes upon her. "I know, how about a garden?"

"A garden," Claire repeated.

"And then in the summer we can come here with the baby . . ."

Chloe hopped up and down. "I want to help, I want to help!"

Claire joined in her excitement, clapping her hands and twirling about.

"Okay," explained Liselle, "hold hands and we'll make a promise to plant a beautiful garden . . ."

"But no vegetables!" exclaimed Claire.

"Silly, you have to have vegetables in a garden," Chloe corrected her.

"No you don't!"

"Yes, you do!"

"Girls, let's make our promise," Liselle stopped their argument as she sang, "ring around the garden, a pocket full of flowers, sunshine and rain, we all fall down . . ."

The girls laughed and tumbled until they tired of the game.

Liselle glanced up at the sound of a car door slamming and her heart skipped a beat. Tom? She squinted into the sun to see a tall blond man walking toward her.

"Well hello Geoff Harmeyer," she called.

"Hello Liselle, nice to see you back on the island. Looks like you've been busy."

"Yes," she smiled as her hand strayed to her expanding waist. "You could say that," she agreed.

On impulse Geoff knelt by the girls and told them to close their eyes. They laughed delightedly when he produced a handful of wildflowers.

"What brings you out my way Geoff?"

"I was just visiting mom's grave, you know, up the road at the cemetery."

"Oh that's right. I'm sorry, about Frieda."

"It's okay, we've adjusted, you know. It has been a couple of years."

"Yes. How are you?"

"I just happened to be home, I miss it."

"I certainly understand that, I love it here," Liselle turned her face to the warm sun. "It's so peaceful."

"Maybe you're just a peaceful person, Liselle. How is Tom?"

"He's fine, really, Geoff, just busy," she replied quickly.

∽

After church the next morning, when Geoff again stopped to say hello, Liselle drove to Lucy's. She felt content being in the place she loved with no phones to answer, no schedules to keep, no restless husband. She stopped. Where did that come from?

"Tell him," again the Voice of her soul master. *"His heart is far from me."*

"I know, Lord," she silently agreed.

"You are my witness to him." The presence of the Lord filled her with hope. They would come back soon, she decided for she missed her time on the island, in her father's house and seeing Lucy. Here the girls could create their own memories.

She recalled her blessings: a husband who provided for them, healthy children, her father's cottage, the love and support of dear Lucy, so why did she feel such unease?

Maybe she had stopped looking for the silver lining, as mother had said so long ago.

An unwelcome thought nudged her. Perhaps their memories should include Alaska? No, not yet, the girls are too young.

And definitely not with the baby!

After lunch, Lucy mentioned her earlier tears. "Are you sure something's not bothering you?"

"Marriage is just so complicated, Lucy, I guess more than I imagined."

"Everyone has their ups and downs," Lucy agreed.

"I didn't know anything about Tom's family; now any mention of a visit is a source of friction between us."

Tears welled as she recalled Tom's pressure. Just last week he had started asking again.

Lucy reached to hug her.

"Lucy, you've always been good for me," she let the tears flow. "And Tom isn't around much. I feel like I'm raising the children alone," she continued.

"And with another one on the way, I'm sure your mommy hormones are working overtime. Of course you feel overwhelmed," Lucy agreed.

"Do you believe in the seven-year itch?" Liselle asked.

"You mean after seven years a man looks for excitement?"

"Yes, they start looking at other women . . ."

"Tom wouldn't do that, Liselle. He might be busy with work and not paying much attention, but, no, I don't believe he would ever look at another woman. How could he, when he has you?"

Not convinced by Lucy's analysis, Liselle plunged ahead, "Next year is our seventh anniversary, and I feel his distance. Our relationship is so different from how it began."

"You don't need to worry about that right now," Lucy admonished.

Liselle left shortly after lunch, the sun shining as she sang with Claire and Chloe to keep their minds off their seat restraints.

Pulling into the driveway she punched the garage door opener.

Tom's car was parked inside.

She was surprised that he hadn't tried to call and wondered what his reaction would be. Odd that she should give him unlimited freedom to come and go, yet he expected her to plan and inform him of every move. Somehow it didn't seem equitable.

The girls tumbled through the door, anxious to see him.

"Daddy, daddy!" they yelled, running in the direction of the den.

He met them in the hallway.

"How are my girls!" he exclaimed, scooping them up, one in each arm as they covered his face with kisses.

"Daddy, you should have come!" Claire admonished.

"Yes, daddy, we're going to plant a garden," Chloe chimed in.

Tom looked over the tops of their heads at Liselle.

"Hello? You look tired."

"I'm okay," she explained, moving awkwardly past him into the kitchen.

A twinge of guilt swept him at how uncomfortable she looked.

"You know you should have called before taking off like that!" he said.

"You had clients all afternoon. I don't imagine I would have reached you."

"Oh, hell, you know I left instructions to put your calls through, whatever I'm doing!"

"Can we discuss this later, if you're going to swear?"

"Yeah, sure, come on, baby dolls let's go to the den while mommy gets dinner."

He set the girls down and followed them as they raced on stubby legs to the den. Relaxing in his recliner by the fireplace, he closed his eyes while the girls jumped on the window seat and threw pillows.

They knew his routine and allowed him to rest before pouncing with their books.

"Daddy, look at this picture of flowers," said Claire.

"It looks like the flowers Geoff gave us," chimed Chloe.

The phone's sudden intrusion irritated Liselle. She hadn't been home five minutes and picked up on the second ring.

"May I speak to Tom, please," a young female purred.

"Just a sec," she responded, buzzing him on the intercom.

Getting juice for the girls, iced tea for herself and Tom, as she approached the den she heard him say before hanging up, "Don't call me at home again, I mean it!"

He sounded angry and looking up at her, attempted a smile as she entered with the tray.

"Is something wrong," she asked.

"No, just a nuisance call, nothing important," he said, steamed that Kristyn would even think of calling him at home.

～

After dinner and the girls were in bed, Tom helped with the dishes, amazed at Liselle's energy and how she ran the household. He decided not to argue about her recent foray to the island. She was obviously bored and needed a change of scenery.

"So how is Lucy?" he inquired.

"Oh, fine, fine! I think I disappointed her by not spending Saturday night with her."

"Where . . ." he paused surprised, ". . . where did you stay?"

"I stayed at the cottage with the girls; they love it there and it was fun to be away from phones and appointment books, just kind of roughing it!"

Her eyes sparkled at the memory.

"I don't suppose you thought about your condition, and not having a phone, did you?"

"Oh, Tom, I don't have a *condition*. I'm having a *baby* in two months, and everything is fine."

"And what about Geoff bringing flowers?"

"You know Frieda's son, Geoff. He was visiting his mother's grave; he stopped to play a silly game with the girls."

"Well, you have to look at it from my viewpoint," he expanded. "I'm supposed to take care of you, provide for you . . ."

"And you do that very well," she agreed, "but you certainly can't watch over us every minute! At some point we have to trust God to protect us and the ones we love."

"Yeah, right!"

He threw down the towel and stormed to the den.

～

Finishing in the kitchen, she hung the towels and stood at the patio door to gaze at the immaculately landscaped yard, the carefully manicured trees and flowers.

As her eyes feasted on the terrace roses a tear slid down her cheek at the memory of the lonely cottage.

Planting a garden would be good, reminding that the secret of nature was patience. Everything took time to grow with fruit the reward. She would be patient with her marriage.

It still shook her, though, when Tom lost his temper. She didn't know if she would ever get used to his short fuse; he seemed so far from being the man of peace that God desired.

"I will lift up my eyes unto the hills, from where my help comes," she quoted the psalm as the last rays of sun tipped Mt. Rainier.

≈

From his recliner, Tom aimlessly flicked the remote at the TV. He knew he had over-reacted, but he was tired of her always bringing God into the discussion. He rarely went to church, though they had started marriage that way. Now it was convenient to use work as an excuse to skip.

When he had agreed to attend her church, he had expected something like the orthodox service with its obligatory attendance on holy days–Christmas and Easter.

But her church was different. He didn't know exactly what it was that bothered him. The people were nice, the music enthusiastic; the message interesting. But when the pastor began to talk about personal sacrifice, Tom tuned out. He had experienced plenty of sacrifice as a kid, had paid his dues and definitely wasn't interested in a religion of sacrifice.

Finishing his martini, he returned to stand behind her. "A penny for . . ." he began.

"If you really want to know, I'm sad about us not attending church as a family. What kind of message does that give the children when you don't go?"

He scowled, but he had asked. "What do you want me to do, not work on an important case just because it's Sunday?"

"No, but I think we could at least spend an hour together in church. I know your profession and your practice requires that you put in lots of hours."

"Well, I'm glad you realize that," he said, sliding his arms around her and easing her to him, nuzzling her neck. He loved the feel of her full shape, so womanly and soft and appealing. Not that he planned to keep her pregnant forever. He liked her other shape, too.

"By the way," she added, "I didn't realize you gave out our phone number to clients?"

"What do you mean?" he asked, having forgotten Kristyn.

"That phone call this evening."

"Oh; that was a law student interning with the firm!"

"She sounded pretty familiar with you . . ." Liselle began.

"Don't give it another thought," he interrupted, "Kristyn's just a little pushy when it comes to getting her work assignments."

Nuzzling her shoulder he continued, "So this little baby is due in two months, huh?"

"That's right," the thought made her smile.

He turned her to him, kissed her gently.

"Then we don't have much time to ourselves. Come to bed?"

"What about our church discussion?"

He paused, relented, "I'll go, but I won't like it," he said.

She gazed into his glowing eyes and took a deep breath before she plunged in.

"There is one thing I want you to know about my faith," she began.

"And what's that? That it means everything to you? That you're on good terms with God?" he joked.

"Well, something along those lines. The Lord is everything to me, the air I breathe; the choices I make all orchestrated by Him. I don't know any other way to live," she explained.

"And I wouldn't want to change any of that," he said, taking her hand as they walked up the stairs.

23

THE TWENTIETH OF MARCH was a typical gray day and her mother's birthday. She had been gone six years now and the reminder only added to Liselle's gloom. Tired of being pregnant, she still had a week to go. Tom had left early with a reminder for her to call after the girls had breakfast.

Easing out of bed, she felt a twinge in her lower back. This was not the time for a backache and quickly she showered, brushed her hair into a loose bun, and pulled on maternity leggings and the largest top she could find.

Outside the girls' door she listened. There was no sound and peeking in, she saw that they were sitting at their small table coloring. Backing out she continued downstairs. There was nothing they could harm themselves on there.

At the stair landing, another sharp twinge gripped her and she clutched the railing. This was more than a backache.

When the twinge released, she hurried downstairs to the phone in the den, relieved when Lucy answered.

"Lucy, you'd better come today!"

"Gracious, are you sure? It will take me about two hours to get there."

"I should still be here, I think, though this doesn't feel like last time. I'm going to call Penny just in case."

"I'm on my way," Lucy promised.

Liselle called Penny, the sitter, wanting her there when Tom came home.

~

"Good morning, Synder, Evans & Wells . . ."

"Tom Caribou, please!"

Liselle was doing her best to control the contractions.

"I'm sorry but he left for an early lunch."

"Did he say where?" she asked, concentrating on her deep breathing exercise.

"No, he didn't. I'm sorry ma'am."

She hung up and punched in his cell, called for fifteen minutes with no response. Her back ache had intensified; the contractions now closer together; the doctor's office advising her to go to the hospital.

She punched in Carolyn's number. They had met two years ago at the Mothers of Twins Club.

"Carolyn, can you drive me to the hospital?"

"Yes, of course. Do you want me to stay with you?"

"I'll be okay once I get there."

"What are you doing with the girls?"

"Penny is coming. She should be here any minute."

"Then I'll leave my two at your house."

"Thanks, Carolyn."

Liselle called the girls downstairs and explained that Penny would fix their breakfast and Lucy was coming. Penny arrived a few minutes later.

Their favorite sitter, they raced to let her in as Carolyn arrived with her four-year old twins.

It had been an hour since the first contraction and Liselle was having difficulty controlling the pain. Penny took the foursome upstairs as Carolyn helped her into the car, placing her bag on the back seat.

Liselle leaned her head against the headrest. Where was Tom? He said to call. Another contraction came fast and hard; she gasped and held her breath as beads of sweat formed on her brow.

"Relax and breathe," Carolyn admonished.

"Thank God we're not far from the hospital," Liselle picked up Carolyn's cell to punch in Tom's direct line.

He picked up on the second ring.

"Tom!" He could hear the stress in her voice.

"What's wrong?"

"The baby's coming; Carolyn's driving me to the hospital."

She grimaced in pain.

"Relax, focus," Carolyn admonished.

"I'm on my way!" Tom yelled into the receiver.

Grabbing his coat, he nearly knocked Kristyn down in the doorway.

"Tom," Kristyn began.

"Not now, talk to Alec," he called over his shoulder as he ran for the elevator.

Angry for letting Kristyn talk him into a working lunch, then forgetting to take his phone, he shoved the car into high gear and raced through mid-morning traffic. He should have been there, even if the baby was early.

The twins had been earlier than this.

When he got to the hospital, the Admitting nurse was slow with his paperwork and he felt the pressure to get upstairs. Once she cleared him and instructed him to check in at maternity, he raced down the hall to the labor room.

The floor attendant stopped him.

"May I help you, sir?"

"Yeah," he gasped, "my wife's in there."

He pointed to the labor rooms.

"We only have one patient today and she's in delivery; what's the name?"

"Caribou," he replied, leaning against the wall out of breath. He had put on a few pounds since hanging at the Club.

"In delivery, follow me."

She led him to the prep room to put on surgical blues. The first was too small and he struggled with it.

"I need a larger size," he said.

"Sir, you don't have much time," she admonished.

Tugging the shirt over his shoulders, he grabbed the mask, adjusted it and walked into delivery as the baby slid from Liselle's straining body and into the doctor's hands.

"It's a boy!" the doctor announced.

Tom hurried to take Liselle's limp hand and kissed her forehead as Carolyn slipped quietly into the hall. "We have a son!"

Her tears matched those stinging his eyes as he stroked her damp forehead.

"I'm sorry I was late, I never expected . . ."

"Shush," Liselle placed her finger on his lips. "You got here just in time."

She felt incredibly light and happy, the intense pain of moments before already fading. The birth had gone well and the baby was healthy! And a boy!

≈

With Liselle settled in her room, Tom went downstairs to order roses. Carolyn was sitting patiently in the hall and seeing her he felt guilty.

"Thanks, Carolyn, for filling in for me."

"I wouldn't have missed it. Births are exciting, and since I won't be having any more . . ." her voice trailed off.

"I really appreciate you taking care of Liselle."

"She's a good friend. I think I'll slip in and see her before I go; poor Penny must be a wreck with four toddlers!"

They laughed at the thought and Tom went to telephone his office.

~

Tom returned in the evening to find Liselle sitting up in bed. "Have you seen him yet?" she asked.

"Yes, I stopped by the nursery."

"And how is he?"

"Gorgeous like his mother; I don't care if he is a boy, he's beautiful!"

Liselle giggled with happiness. "And how are the girls?"

"Oh, they wanted to see their little brother right now. Lucy was there and they were having a good time, but they weren't very happy about not getting to come."

"Sweet Lucy; isn't he wonderful, Tom?!"

"Absolutely, when are they bringing him in?"

"In just a few minutes, it's feeding time and we haven't finalized his name."

The door opened and the nurse rolled in the isolette. After verifying mother's and baby's arm bands she carefully placed him in Liselle's waiting arms.

"Baby boy Caribou, March 20, seven lb. two oz.," Liselle read. "Born on my mother's birthday, who would have guessed?"

Tom gazed at the wheat-colored fuzz sticking up on the tiny head as his son squinted to open blue eyes.

"Well, he needs a special name for this day," Tom began.

"I would like to call him Henry after my father."

"And my brother," Tom agreed.

Liselle winced at her insensitivity.

"Henry Tomas Caribou," she rolled the name off her tongue. "How does that sound?"

"It sounds excellent," he agreed, "That makes him the second Henry Caribou. Hello little guy."

When Liselle finished feeding him, Tom went home to put the girls to bed.

~

Lucy entered Liselle's room, walking two feet off the floor and greeted Liselle with a kiss and more roses.

"What do you think of your grand cousin?"

"He's perfect! And to think he had to hurry and be born on your mother's birthday!"

"Yes, a pleasant surprise."

Liselle thought how special this day would always be, the birthday of two special people; her mother and her son.

"And he has a fine name," Lucy continued. "Henry Tomas, little Hank!"

Liselle's heart overflowed with happiness and she rested well that night, determined to go home the next day. She missed the girls and they missed her.

Besides, the birth had been uneventful and she decided that single births were much easier.

~

Walking through the doors of Synder, Evans & Wells the next morning, Tom was greeted with congratulations. He had scheduled a meeting with Bill Shank, the managing partner, to discuss reassigning Kristyn. She was a nuisance and he wasn't getting any work done with her constant interruptions.

Leaving Bill's office and walking back to his own, he scowled when he saw Kristyn waiting for him.

"Congratulations, dad!" she teased.

"Kristyn, we need to talk," he said.

She looped her arm through his as they entered his office.

"Sure, boss, whatever you say," she began, as he closed the door.

"Sit down, Kristyn. First of all, I'm not your boss . . ."

"Well, sure you are. You handle my assignments . . ."

"Not anymore!"

"Excuse me?" she stammered.

"You've been reassigned to bankruptcy . . ."

"I don't want to do bankruptcy. That's not the kind of law I like," she argued.

"If you remember," he explained, "we have a requirement that interns study three areas of law. I'm sure that was explained when you started. You've completed contracts and estate planning; domestic isn't ready to rotate, bankruptcy can use your help," he explained.

"But I haven't finished the litigation we were working on."

"Close enough for government work," he said. "Besides I think you'll find that bankruptcy requires a great deal of research."

He handed her a file.

"Here's a start; check with Frank Herron this afternoon for the rest of your assignment."

"Oh, not Frank!" she wailed. "Come on, Tom, what's wrong with me working for you a little longer? I thought we had a good thing going?"

"In case you haven't noticed, I'm a very busy partner in this law firm, I've given your new assignment, and that's final."

He moved to open the door.

She glared as she stood.

"I never thought you would pull rank, Tom, I never thought that would happen!"

He opened his mouth to respond, changed his mind as she rushed past him, and called after her retreating form, "Tell Frank I said hi."

Relieved that was over, he never figured Kristyn would put up a fuss. In his opinion she flirted with everyone. He cringed to think how easily he had let a young woman sway him into an involvement that would have jeopardized his marriage.

He resolved to work harder, be home more. If he had to burn the midnight oil after the kids were asleep, that's the way it was going to be and picking up the latest pleadings in his in-box, he worked another hour before going to the hospital to take Liselle and little Henry home.

24

BY LATE AFTERNOON LISELLE was settled in the den with bassinet beside her, Claire and Chloe hanging on either side adoring their baby brother. Tom relaxed in his easy chair with the television on low as wonderful smells wafted from the kitchen with Lucy preparing a feast.

When all was on the table, Lucy rolled the bassinet into the dining room while Tom helped Liselle walk to her chair to sit carefully, stiffly.

The phone rang and Lucy went to answer.

When she returned, Tom looked at her with inquiring eyes.

"Some woman said to tell you she can't make it tonight."

Tom scowled as Liselle looked at him inquiringly. It had to be Kristyn playing a joke. What in the world was she thinking?

"It must be a mistake," he said. "I don't have any plans for tonight!"

Just then Henry let out a lusty wail, and everyone's attention turned to the bassinet.

"Thanks pal," he muttered as Lucy hurried to pick him up.

∼

Henry slept through the first night, then had his nights and days mixed up. With his bassinet beside their bed, sleep was sporadic.

Tom moved into the guest room for his early morning meetings, though he preferred his room. When he did stay the night, he sometimes woke to catch a glimpse of Liselle nursing Henry, the most precious part of his life.

After the first month, Liselle moved Henry to his own room but many mornings Tom would tiptoe over to kiss her goodbye and discover Henry curled sleepily in her arms. He loved to see them this way.

With the girls, it hadn't been so easy, caring for two at once and Liselle had hired a nanny. Now he urged her to do the same but she insisted on a nanny only two days a week. She didn't want the girls to feel pushed aside or ignored.

As Tom entered his office one morning, he saw Alec walking down the hall and stopped to greet him. "Hey stranger, you're here pretty early!"

"So are you, how you doing, Tom?"

"Good, how about yourself?"

Alec smiled and turned serious.

"Did you hear about Kristyn?"

"No," Tom frowned, "what's up?"

"She was let go! There's a rumor that she and one of the partners got involved; wife found out. The big guys got her out of here as fast as they could."

Tom stared at him, dumbfounded. "Why are you telling me?" he asked.

Alec shifted his weight uncomfortably and rubbed his neck.

"Actually, Tom, to tell you the truth; don't get mad, I was afraid . . ."

"That it was me?" Tom demanded.

Alec nodded as a flush spread across his face.

"I think I'm smarter than that," Tom defended.

"Look Tom, I know she was coming on to you, and let's face it, Kristyn is attractive. Besides, 'smart' doesn't have a lot to do with it. You get a chick like that messing around."

"So where did she go?" Tom asked.

"Who knows? That's all I heard."

"Well keep me posted, man," Tom said as he entered his office, scowling and picking up a file to review.

He had trouble concentrating. Kristyn wasn't a bad person, a little mixed up maybe, looking for love like everyone else.

He called the florist and ordered flowers for Liselle. More than ever, he wanted to spend his life with her, grow old with her, yet it seemed that marriages all around were crumbling, marriages that looked like they were on solid ground. God, what did it take to keep it going in the right direction? Liselle seemed happy enough, but what if she wasn't?

He would plan to be home for dinner.

Liselle opened the door to the florist and pleasantly surprised, hurriedly stuck the roses in the refrigerator. Henry was wailing upstairs and the girls tugged on her robe, arguing over a favorite toy. It was nanny's day off; perhaps she had been too hasty in limiting her hours.

By mid-afternoon the girls were settled in their room and the baby snoozed. Quickly she dressed. What to fix for dinner. She looked in the freezer, only to find chicken quiche. That would have to do; besides her energy was gone.

She popped the quiche in the oven as she heard Tom's car pull in the garage.

It was then she remembered his roses, still in their box.

Pulling them out and rummaging under the sink for a vase, she began trimming the lower stems and jabbed her thumb on a thorn as Tom walked in.

"Hi darling, I see you got my roses."

Liselle sucked her injured thumb.

"Did they just come?" he asked, surprised.

"Oh, Tom, what a day for flowers!" she began.

"Here let me do that for you," he offered. "Sit on the stool and tell me about it."

He was tired too, but not as tired as she looked and gratefully, she obeyed.

"What happened?"

"It was nanny's day off and I got a bit overwhelmed."

"And why didn't you get somebody else?"

"I feel like I'm spoiled. I want to do it myself!"

"And what did this teach you?" he demanded.

"I can manage but I'm a wreck by dinner. I'm afraid all you're getting is chicken quiche–oh no!"

She rushed to the oven and pulled out a smoking blackened pie.

"And what is this," he teased, "Cajun cooking?"

He laughed heartily; then stopped at her tears.

"C'mon, Liselle, I'll order Chinese, give Henry his bath and read to the girls."

His concern made her weep noisily.

"Here, here, what are these tears about?"

He held her close and she leaned into his comforting arms.

"Why don't you go relax in a nice hot tub," he suggested.

"What about the kids?" she asked.

"I can handle these kids for an hour," he boasted. "After all, you do it all day! 'Course if Henry gets hungry I'll have to bring him to you. I'm not plumbed for that!"

She laughed and he joined her, relieved to see a smile return to her face.

∽

Later that evening he fell asleep in the den, completely exhausted from his early morning and the evening at home. Gently, Liselle kissed him awake.

"Thank you," she said.

"For . . . ?"

"For being here . . ."

"Sure," he said, snuggling into his recliner.

"Come to bed, you won't sleep well here."

"I'm okay."

She tugged on his arm until he stirred awake and followed her up the stairs. The warm soak had done wonders for her energy and snuggling between the sheets she wrapped her arms around him and stroked the gray beginning to show at his temples. She wanted him to know she appreciated his help but he fell asleep in her arms, mumbling that he loved her.

∽

Liselle woke in a cold sweat, the third time she'd had the same dream. *Alone in a freezing wind by her parents' graves, she counted three headstones but couldn't read the third name; in the distance a child cried.*

Tom touched her shoulder, "Are you having a bad dream?"

"I think so."

"You were restless," he explained.

She sat up, anxious to change the subject.

"Whatever happened to that young intern you worked with," she asked.

"Oh, Kristyn; she got busted," he smiled.

"Busted, how?"

"Seems she had an affair with one of the partners; wife found out. She was gone before it got messy."

"Oh," Liselle was puzzled.

"I would never do that to you," he assured.

"I would hope not," she replied, recalling how often he vowed his faithfulness. "It would be the end of our marriage, Mr. Caribou, a real deal breaker."

At her words, his stomach twisted in knots.

25

IT WAS SPRINGTIME AND time to plant the garden. Liselle was taking the kids to the island on Monday and Tom would join them on Saturday for the weekend. The girls helped Liselle pack and played with Hank while she got the cooler ready and loaded the trusty jeep that she refused to trade in.

The car fit her like a comfy pair of shoes and if the girls got sand in the back seat, or spilled a drink on the worn cushions, it was not the end of the world as it would be in Tom's car.

～

Tom was at the office working through a pile of paperwork. With a new paralegal to train, new clients to counsel and a late dinner meeting on Friday, it would be tight but he should make it to the island by Saturday.

Kelly knocked lightly before entering.

"Come," he said and paused to study her long black hair, almond shaped eyes, and divine young body showcased in tight sweater and short leather skirt. Her exotic looks reminded of Nedelia except she was sophisticated in a way Nedelia would never be. Nevertheless, his physical reaction to her was the same.

The first and only time he had taken Liselle to Alaska, he had forced himself to ignore Nedelia, especially since she was married to his brother. But she still had a powerful effect on him, though marriage to her would never have worked. She was old-world and would never leave the island, their stolen moments a distant memory. It was better the way it had worked out.

Now Kelly's looks stirred memories and when Liselle said she would be gone all week, fear had risen in Tom's chest. Alone in the house was more than he could stand.

He pushed their last conversation from his mind when she promised divorce if he were ever unfaithful. God, she must never find out about Kristyn. It should be easy to ignore Kelly. Having hired her as his new paralegal, he was determined to avoid her.

"Mr. Caribou?"

"Huh? Oh, Tom, call me Tom."

He smiled, his eyes resting on the outline of her breasts and seeing his interest, she sat down, crossed her legs and leaned forward.

"What case would you like me to start on?"

"How about lunch," he said. "And we can discuss our strategy."

And that's the way it went, each day they worked until 6:00, dined at the Club and spent evenings at her apartment, Tom fantasizing that she was Nedelia with her silky hair spread over her naked shoulders and slim legs entwining him.

One night an image of Liselle suddenly came to his mind and gulping his martini, he dressed and left, leaving Kelly to wonder at his sudden flight.

～

He finished with clients late on Friday night and Saturday morning raced to Steilacoom in his new Italian sports car. The beautiful powerful machine amazed and delighted him and fit him so well, confirming the fast track he was on. He felt invincible and caught the noon ferry with time to spare.

Liselle looked relieved when he pulled up to the mansion. "You made it," she greeted with Hank asleep on her shoulder.

Half-heartedly he hugged her and reached to pat the baby's downy head.

Stepping back, she looked at him.

He had loosened his tie and rolled up his shirt sleeves. With more gray at his temples, a little paunch at his waist, dark circles had pooled under his eyes.

"A weekend of rest will do you good," she said. "Nice car."

"Oh yeah, my latest bonus," he explained. "It was delivered this week."

"You mean it was a surprise," she asked, putting Hank in his bassinet.

"Uh, no, I knew it was coming, just didn't know when."

He frowned as he followed her into the dining room.

"Lunch is ready," Lucy said, hugging him and placing a bowl of chowder before him.

"We're staying at Lucy's, right?" he asked.

"The girls were hoping to sleep at the cottage," Liselle explained.

Claire and Chloe smiled expectantly. "Daddy, we want you to see our garden," they chimed.

"Well, I'm too tired," he grumbled.

"Girls, daddy wants to sleep at Lucy's tonight," Liselle explained. "He worked hard all week; we can see the garden tomorrow."

Her heart ached at the disappointment on their little faces. Why was he so careless about their feelings; couldn't he see what he was doing?

Excusing himself, he walked to the bathroom as guilt swept and panic flooded his chest. Disaster loomed, he was headed for the wall and didn't know how to stop his headlong plunge into it.

He had achieved power and success, but felt empty inside. Now one wrong move or one bit of bad luck and everything would come crashing down.

Splashing cold water on his face, he returned to the dining room. All eyes followed him as he walked to the credenza, poured bourbon and downed it in one gulp.

Ignoring them, he slammed out the door.

Liselle followed. "Tom, what's wrong?"

"With . . . ?"

"You seem really wound up."

"Just work pressures," he explained.

"You know you don't have to work so hard. We have everything we need."

"Ye-a-ah, and how do you expect to keep it," he asked.

"What do you mean?"

"We don't own anything," he explained. "We have a huge mortgage that I have to put in 80 hours a week to pay, not to mention the kids' college and everything else."

"I think you should take a small vacation with us," she offered. "Just two weeks. It will do wonders for you."

He slumped on the porch steps as she massaged his shoulders. This was perfect timing.

"Actually," he began, "I was meaning to tell you about Ivan's wedding next month."

"What? You never mentioned it," she was shocked.

"You knew he was getting married," he turned the discussion back on her.

"I knew he was getting married *some* day; I thought I would have more notice than a few weeks."

She was hurt by his lack of communication. The girls were three, Hank barely 4 months. Surely he didn't intend to take them.

"How long have you known . . . ?"

"Not too long," he lied.

"I think it would be fine for you to attend," she agreed. "We'll send a really nice gift so Ivan knows I'm sorry to miss it."

"What are you talking about? We are all going," he ordered.

"I'm not going and neither is the baby. What if he gets sick?"

"I survived and so will he."

"We're not going and that's all there is to it."

She went back inside; her face flushed and tears stinging her eyes.

Lucy put her arms around her. "Liselle, are you sure?"

"Lucy, you haven't seen how they live. I mean there are bugs in the walls, and–and mice! The floor is dirt, the food is oily. It makes me nauseated. And it's a ferry to get there after a bumpy commuter flight. No, it's out of the question."

The sudden squeal of tires startled them and they looked out the window to see Tom's tail-lights disappearing in a cloud of dust.

"You see what I'm up against?" she cried. "If everything doesn't go his way, he gets mad and leaves."

"I didn't know," Lucy apologized. "I've never seen Tom like this."

"It seems to be a permanent condition, in fact," Liselle exclaimed as truth dawned, "I think he hates this island as much as I dislike his."

~

Liselle hummed as she straightened the bureau in their bedroom. After the last few months of short nights and long days, it felt good to have her energy back. The girls were in their playroom and Hank napped on her bed as she thought about the evening before when Tom had shown her the airline tickets, pointing out their exorbitant price.

She knew he meant it as coercion for she would never waste money. Perhaps a quick trip to Alaska was not such a big deal. She would trust God to take care of them, as He always did. And it would be nice for Tom's parents to meet their newest grandson.

Determined to be positive about Ivan's wedding, she lifted a stack of papers from the dresser to move to Tom's desk in the den. As she did, a cream-colored envelope sailed to the carpet and she stooped to retrieve it, shocked to see it was postmarked Dutch Harbor from three months ago.

With trembling hands she opened the envelope and read the wedding invitation.

Tom had known for months and hadn't bothered telling her!

Carefully she placed the papers back on the dresser as the temper she thought she had under control surfaced with sudden ferocity. She didn't care if Tom had paid an exorbitant price for tickets, enough of his secrets and control. It was wrong to not give her adequate time to prepare, the money be damned.

She picked up the phone to make other plans.

The morning of their trip Liselle was up early as Tom readied for work, once again explaining the schedule to her. "We'll meet at the airport at 10:00, our flight leaves at noon. That gets us into St. Paul by early evening. The kids will sleep and the wedding is the next day."

He kissed her check. "We come home the following day you know, the ferry runs every other day."

She said nothing but once she heard the garage door close, flew into action. Having packed wedding attire for Tom; for herself and the children she had packed differently and placing their luggage in the car, the kids strapped in their seats, she backed down the driveway.

The flight for her and the children left for Seattle at 8:30 where they would meet Lucy and drive to the Mukilteo ferry. From there it was 20 minutes to a weekend on Whidbey Island.

Deplaning at 9:30 and walking through the Seattle terminal, Liselle punched in Tom's number, relieved when it went to his voicemail. Quickly she left a message.

"Tom, you need to go home for your luggage, I'm not meeting you at the airport as the children and I will be elsewhere for the weekend and my phone will be *off*."

Spotting Lucy, she handed Henry to her and turned off her cell phone before tossing it into a bag. Taking the girls' hands they walked to baggage claim and Liselle sighed with relief when their suitcases came down the chute.

With Lucy's rental car waiting, she smiled and said, "Let the fun begin!"

~

Tom glanced at his watch for the fifth time and punched in his home number. Why wasn't she picking up? As he slowly closed his flip phone, this time he heard the message waiting beep, punched in his code and listened in stunned silence before slamming the phone shut, the color draining from his face.

She had left him. How could she do this?

~

Lucy and Liselle made the weekend an adventure, visiting Oak Harbor, lunching at Whidbey State Park, as Liselle tried to avoid thinking about going home and what that might mean.

She snapped lots of pictures but her favorite was the girls running through a field of lavender with the sunlight in their hair. Even if the picture didn't turn out, the day would be forever seared in her memory.

They walked the beach and laughed in delight when Henry tried to crawl, her heart aching that Tom had missed it. She wondered if he felt the same joy in his children as she did.

On the final evening as Lucy napped in the leather recliner Liselle tiptoed to the porch and gazed at the sunset.

She was tired too, Claire in time-out more than usual while Chloe had been the perfect child. She remembered the times when she had been incorrigible and mother had promised one day she would have a child like herself. Claire was definitely it.

In the evening stillness the crickets sang while she reflected on the years since mother's death; remembered how upset she had been during their courtship when Tom didn't call, how it had mattered, how hard she tried to please him, wanted to spend time with him.

Was it just the challenge of courtship that had driven him to marry her, the fact that she was hard to get? Did he love her? Did he know what love was?

She knew nothing of his past relationships except for Nedelia, and at that she could only guess. He never mentioned other women; somehow his past never came up.

She trusted him completely, perhaps only seeing the man she wanted him to be. Now obvious cracks had surfaced in their relationship and questions floated through her mind like disturbed cobwebs. What was he really about? He tried to control everything and by doing so, assumed everything was splendid. Well, it definitely was not and now he knew.

She wasn't proud of what she had done, deserting him like that. She believed in treating others as she wanted to be treated and leaving him to face his family alone, even though he did that to her, still felt wrong.

She pushed down her fear of the future. She wanted her children to have a happy childhood with two parents but what were her choices? Move back with Lucy or stay and battle it out?

She had no idea how Tom would react for she had never defied him before. He knew how to argue, how to win, but the real issue was protecting the children. They deserved a good father, and he was a good father.

The fact remained that she would never jeopardize their health or safety by taking them to Alaska. Not while they were small, but was she risking their future happiness now? With heavy heart, she prayed for God to change Tom's heart.

She heard Lucy stirring behind her. They had grown close, sharing their faith, the closest of confidantes and as a grandmother figure to her children, Liselle relied on Lucy's good opinions.

"What are you going to do when you see Tom?" Lucy asked from her chair.

"Oh, I'm sure I'll think of something," Liselle answered quickly.

"I'm serious, Liselle. He's not going to be happy with you abandoning him for Ivan's wedding."

"I know, as I was sitting here reviewing my options, I thought about the inscription on Grandmother's headstone. Do you remember it?"

"Not right this minute," Lucy confessed.

"It said: *I wish you enough loss to appreciate all you have.* My losses have taught me to do that, I only hope Tom sees it the same way. I have allowed him to control everything. He doesn't ask, never has; just makes plans and I fall into line. Our lack of communication backfired this time and I pray we can work this out and move forward together, but on new terms and with different rules."

~

On Sunday they visited a peacock farm, the showy birds roaming freely and spreading their luxurious plumage, delighting the twins.

At the Mukilteo ferry they grabbed a quick lunch at Ivar's Seafood Bar before heading for the Seattle airport, the girls playing with their stuffed peacocks while Henry watched from his car seat.

"Call me tomorrow, Liselle, and if you need anything, you know I'll be there," Lucy promised. "Or if you just need a quiet place to stay."

"I know, thank you Lucy."

Lucy departed first while Liselle checked in. Unless Tom changed his flight, he would be home today. It was possible he would stay longer and part of her hoped that he would so she didn't have to face him tonight.

26

I sing in the shadow of your wings.

PSALM 63:7

LISELLE PULLED INTO THE driveway and punched the garage door opener. Tom's car was not there and she sighed with relief. Remembering to turn on her cell phone, there were no messages from him either. Good, perhaps he had come to terms with what she needed.

"Lord God, help me say the right things and not act in anger," she prayed as she unlocked the door and turning the knob, Henry in her arms and the girls trailing behind, she opened the door and came face to face with Tom.

Gasping, she turned pale. "Tom! I wasn't expecting you."

"No, my love, I don't imagine you were. Come in." He took Henry from her.

"Where's your car?"

"In the shop, Alec brought me home."

"What happened to your car?" she struggled to regain her composure.

"That's not important right now. We need to talk," he declared angrily.

Henry squirmed and reached for her while the girls began to cry.

"The kids are tired, can't this wait?"

With great effort, he composed himself. "Come girls, say hi to daddy," he encouraged. They went with him to the kitchen while Liselle soothed Henry.

It was a quiet, strained evening. Feeding the kids, putting them to bed, warily she watched him.

~

Later, soaking in the bathtub, she heard the bedroom door open and Tom appeared with a mug of hot chocolate. Placing it beside her, he sat on the edge of the tub and stared at her. She felt totally vulnerable, not knowing if she should stay in the tub or get out.

"You made me look bad to my family," he began.

"This is not just about you, you know," she responded hotly.

Dropping his head, he agreed, "I know. I don't want us to be apart. I've been doing a lot of thinking."

She reached for her hot chocolate and attempted to lighten the mood.

"Ummm, this is good, I didn't know you could cook."

"Fine, rub it in that I don't help you enough," he retorted.

Tears spilled down her cheeks and sobbing, she reached for her towel and stood to dry. He grabbed her and pulled her firmly to him, kissing her passionately on the mouth.

"You know I hate to see you cry. And I know I'm not the husband you deserve."

She hugged him back, kissing the tears on his face. As she wrapped her legs around him, he lifted her and carried her to their bed. It was the most passionate, intimate moment of their marriage, his soul bare before her. He did care about her, about their marriage.

Exhausted and content, she fell asleep in his arms and stroking her hair, he whispered, "There is something I need to tell you."

But she was out for the night.

~

In the dim morning light, sitting in the kitchen with coffee and morning paper, Tom wondered at his lack of judgment the night before. What had possessed him to want to confess all? She had promised a divorce if he was ever unfaithful.

And he would be lost without her, her sudden flight shaking him to his core. He had thought to confess all and start over, but as much as he wanted to clear everything, his infidelity—no, adultery—call it what it was, had to remain his sad, sorry secret. She could never forgive that. Nor did he expect her to. She was too trusting, too sweet, to absorb the sordid mess of his betrayal.

He heard the first gentle sounds of the piano and basked in Liselle's recital, each note resonating sweetly, deeply in his weary spirit as he recognized the song from his youth.

It stirred memories as he recalled the words: "*Jesus loves me, this I know, for the Bible tells me so.*"

Reflecting on the simplicity of the message, its power reached him, stunned him. "*Little ones to him belong, they are weak, but he is strong*".

He was fluent in three languages, had studied the law and the writings of great minds, yet didn't know the Bible. His little girls knew more about it than he did. How was that possible?

How easily he had overlooked the obvious. His wife was a Believer, while he had only mouthed the words. Unfaithful to her and to God, the sacrifice he had so long sought to avoid had been merely to deny those things that would destroy his happiness. And at that he had failed miserably.

Closing his eyes he listened to her continuing recital. He knew it was how she worshipped, segueing from nursery songs to praise hymns and finally the doxology: "*Praise God from whom all blessings flow.*"

"Jesus, help me, forgive me," he prayed, "I've been such a fool."

He sat with his eyes closed until Liselle entered the room.

"There you are," she said, leaning to kiss him.

He reached for her hand. "There's something I want to tell you," he said.

At her expectant look, he continued. "I really want to attend church with you and the kids. No more going without me. What you have with God is important. I want that in my life, too."

Tom had promised to be home for dinner and Liselle spent a quiet afternoon fixing his favorite dishes, interrupted once when Hank rushed in to say he lost some teeth.

"Look, mom!" Proudly he held up his treasures, 3 pearly white teeth.

"Hank, you're only four! You're too young to lose teeth."

"I did, mom, really," he insisted.

Kneeling on the floor, she peered in his mouth. "Show me where, honey."

"Way in back," he insisted.

"Baby, are you telling me the truth?"

At her question, he burst into tears and wrapping her arms around him, she dried his face.

"Hank, why are you making this up?"

"Claire said I would get money from the tooth fairy."

"So where did you find the teeth," she asked.

"Next door, the puppy lost them," he explained.

"Okay, back out to play, I will deal with Claire later."

Liselle chuckled to herself, how cute to think they could fool her with puppy teeth; Tom would have a good laugh.

~

Tom arrived promptly at 6:00 and surprised her with roses. Her smile filled her face as she removed the card; then puckered into a frown as she read it and stared at him, her eyes stormy.

"A cruise to Alaska, is this a joke?"

"No, it's not what you think," he hastened to sooth her. "Cruising is really the only way to appreciate such a beautiful wild place. I don't know why I didn't think of it before. You'll like it, really, trust me," he said.

At her silent puzzled look, he continued: "We have a balcony suite, the formal dining is superb, and Lucy has agreed to watch the kids . . . a whole week alone."

~

Liselle did love it and was enchanted with Ketchikan, Skagway and Juneau where they took a plane ride over glaciers slashed with ribbons of turquoise and rafted down the Cirkott River. In Ketchikan she marveled at the brightly colored houses and fishing boats. What a pretty picture to paint, she thought as her fear of Alaska's great unpopulated stretches melted away. She marveled at the blending of cultures and the wild solitary beauty.

And of course there was nothing disagreeable on the ship, everything designed to please and pamper. Their relationship bonded, a week of dining and dancing, attending shows every night with leisurely swims and day trips ashore.

Once back home, as she hung the artwork they had purchased in Juneau, Liselle reflected on how most people left their memories behind when they moved. Hers went with her and now hung on their walls, beautiful reminders of places they had visited. Even the collage she had made with Lucy on their first Christmas hung in the den during the holidays.

~

Gradually she could sense little changes in Tom; he was more receptive to her ideas, waited to discuss a topic with her rather than just take charge. Their lives weren't perfect, but the relationship was good and peaceful. And the kids were secure in a loving home with two parents, active in sports and church. The time seemed to fly as the girls finished junior high and Hank started sixth grade.

Since Lucy no longer traveled to Olympia, Liselle made frequent trips to Anderson, often with the kids. Sometimes the kids stayed home and Tom adjusted his schedule. A measure of contentment settled upon them.

Each summer one child went to stay with Lucy for a week while the other two accompanied Liselle to the orchards. It was good experience for them, earning money while learning to appreciate the outdoors.

Strawberries were the first crop each spring, picking them backbreaking and tedious as each stubborn stem required removal. Next were cherries, this time the flimsy stems had to stay on, the kids climbing rickety ladders to the treetops, stopping at noon to eat their sack lunches, returning home wiry and tanned.

Peach season, the most delicate crop, had to be carefully placed in crates and they worked the rows together filling their daily quotas. For bean harvest, Liselle only took them for a few days since there was no shade in the fields. After that they had the month of August to swim or hang out with friends before school started.

Tom no longer asked to visit Alaska. Instead, he invited his family to Olympia; Ivan the only one to come with his wife. Tom still hoped to one day take the children so they could appreciate his childhood and all that they had in Olympia.

Liselle visited Anderson as often as possible but rarely stayed at the cottage, not wanting to leave Lucy alone. When Lucy took her afternoon nap, Liselle walked to the cottage where she would sit and reflect on how a photo and a pendant had changed the direction of her life.

On one such visit, as she tended the small garden that was mostly weeds, the sun warmed her and peace rose in her heart, finding expression in a tune. She was humming softly when a shadow fell across her path.

"Oh, Geoff, you startled me," she exclaimed.

"You just can't stay away from this place, can you?" he inquired.

"No, I guess not. I love the island."

"And Tom doesn't?" he asked

"I wouldn't say that."

"Seems like it to me, he never comes."

"It's different, a part of me will always be here; besides, I don't really care for his frozen little island either! It's a mutual understanding," she laughed.

"Well, you should dump him and marry me," Geoff teased.

Liselle laughed more heartily than before, her face lighting with happiness.

"That would make everything perfect," she joked.

Geoff leaned down and kissed her.

She recoiled, horrified.

"Geoff, you can't do that. I'm a married woman with three children!"

"You never even gave me a chance, marrying Tom so fast. You and I are more suited to each other!" he exclaimed. "And I won't apologize for kissing you!"

Angrily she marched with hoe to the back of the cottage. "What you are saying is ridiculous; that's the end of it!" she retorted.

As he reached for her again, she brandished the hoe in his face. "Don't ever touch me again, and stay off my property, too!"

"Okay, okay," he backed away. "Wow, you're different from other women," he said in parting.

Inside the cottage Liselle slumped in the kitchen chair. What was that all about?

She decided not to mention Geoff's behavior to anyone and saying good-bye to Lucy drove back to Olympia. She had her mind on other things. Lucy's health not good, she debated moving her to Olympia, but the move might be too much. She would ask Tom.

Pulling into the garage, she entered through the long back corridor to a quiet house.

"Hello, I'm home! Where is everyone?"

"Hi, mom, we're in the den," called Hank.

The kids were bent over their school work, Tom asleep in the recliner.

Opening his eyes, he asked, "How's my best girl?"

"Great, do I smell roast?" she asked.

"Uh-huh, the girls are teaching me to cook," he offered.

"Oh, daddy, you know how to cook," said Claire.

"I made the pie," offered Chloe.

"Well I better check the kitchen then," Liselle replied.

∾

After dinner and clean up, lights out early for school the next day, Tom snuggled close to Liselle. He continued to pray that she would someday be able to hear and forgive his indiscretions. He was deeply sorry for each one and guilt stalked his soul while a sword hung over his head.

"I never told you, did I, that you're the only woman who ever made me feel so incredible after love-making," he said.

Remembering Geoff's seductive kiss, Tom's attempt at romance failed miserably and she sat up in bed.

"How many women are we talking about?"

"What?" Tom asked drowsily.

"How many women have you been with," she repeated.

"What are you talking about?" Tom was now fully awake.

"You just compared me to 'other women,'" she replied, confused and shaking.

"I'm not talking about other women, I'm talking about you," he explained.

"Who am I being compared with," she demanded.

"Liselle, are you getting hormonal on me?"

"Don't change the subject." Now she was upset.

"Let's just go to sleep," he replied. "Maybe we can start over in the morning."

She lay awake until midnight, puzzled over his remarks, Geoff's action stirring some long buried fear in her.

∾

The next morning after Tom left for work Liselle moved around the kitchen, fixing lunches, straightening up; hurrying the kids out the door to school. When the house was quiet and she was alone, she reached for her Bible on the table in the study.

Questions loomed. Maybe she was the naive one, growing up without a father and having dated few men. Maybe all men acted like Geoff, his actions so unexpected. Had he ever married, was he looking for a little action on the island? Perhaps he thought Tom wasn't attentive enough.

She had never discussed Geoff with Lucy, didn't know what he had done over the years, but in her own mind, of this she was certain; she could never forgive an adulterous husband. Nor did God ask her to. The Bible was clear that an unfaithful spouse was grounds for divorce.

As she searched scripture seeking to justify her position, she began to see other words that hinted of a deeper love, and a deeper sin than she had considered as God's grace jumped off the pages at her. The master forgave his servant a great debt . . . then the servant threw another in prison for a much smaller debt. Matthew 18:32–33 *"Shouldn't you have had mercy on your fellow servant just as I had mercy on you?"*

Ideas filled her mind; bits of teaching from different scriptures flooded her memory and she struggled to keep her thoughts from getting lost. Was she proud?

James 4:6 caught her eye: *"But he gives us more grace. That is why scripture says 'God opposes the proud but gives grace to the humble',"*

Matthew 10:24: *"The servant is not greater than the Master."*

He forgave the woman caught in adultery. Luke 6:36 jumped out at her: *'be merciful, just as your Father is merciful'.*

Was she merciful? Bowing her head and ready to face the unthinkable, she asked, "Lord, has Tom been unfaithful? I pray it is not so, but I ask for your guidance and wisdom. And I confess that I am in need of your mercy."

She felt guilty for doubting her husband. He said he would never be unfaithful, so why was she even thinking this way? The Lord's presence filled her and she hummed as she did the laundry. They were okay, sure they were.

27

When we were overwhelmed by sins,
you forgave our transgressions.

PSALM 65:3

WORKING DILIGENTLY ON A difficult file, last night's conversation with Liselle eons away at the moment, Tom was interrupted by a knock on the door and gruffly he answered, "Come in!"

Kristyn stood before him, decked out to show her physical attributes. After all this time, she still looked good, though he hadn't seen her since she left the firm years ago.

"Kristyn, how are you?" he called.

"Hey, Tom, ole' buddy, I'm doing fine," she responded and not waiting for an invitation, draped herself on the arm of a chair and closed the door with her heeled foot.

"I'm rather busy, Kristyn, what can I do for you?"

"Oh, I would say you can do a lot for me, Tom, what with all this money you're making, your position here in the firm, et cetera!"

"How's that," he asked.

"I'll be brief, Tom. You always were a good lover. I imagine, like wine, you've gotten better with age. So, you can set me up in an apartment and we can start where we left off or . . ."

"Those days are over for me, Kristyn," Tom said.

"Hang on there, pal, I'm not finished," she interrupted. "Scenario numero dos, you can just make monthly payments and we can skip the sex part. Either way, makes no difference to me," she finished.

"Like I said, those days are long gone."

He stood to open the door.

She slammed it with her foot.

"Then you leave me no choice but to go to your wife, Tomas," she threatened.

"It's your word against mine," he said.

"Except that I've taped this entire conversation, pal, so I'm pretty sure your wife would have a hard time believing we didn't get it on, get my drift?" she asked.

His face turned pale.

"I need some time to think," he whispered hoarsely.

"Hey, I'll give you to next Monday, this being such a big decision." Her sarcasm stung as she continued, "I can spare that much time, but that's all. The rent is due and I have some real serious needs right now."

She looked him in the eye before she sauntered out, swinging her hips.

Tom finished dictating the stack of files and left work early to drive around aimlessly in his latest bonus, a pearl white beamer convertible with gold accents and grey leather interior. Mentally he replayed Kristyn's conversation.

Everything was coming down. If he paid her off, what kind of person did that make him–and her? He would be tied to her in an unholy scheme; nasty and distasteful. Blackmail was always ugly with no winners.

If he confessed to Liselle and defused Kristyn's blackmail attempts, he stood to lose everything that was dear to him, his wife, his kids and his community standing.

He had already lost his self-respect.

He thought of all the money he had made over the years, the fast cars, hot babes, fancy meals with two-martini lunches. He would give it all up now if it meant life could go on with Liselle.

He remembered the pastor's message on Sunday from Mark 8:36: "What good is it for a man to gain the whole world, yet lose his own soul?"

Liselle was his soul, the very heart of his life. Maybe he hadn't realized it before, but a certain truth now slapped him in the face. The thing he had been running from all this time loomed before him and he was about to lose.

There was no way he could avoid telling Liselle and soon, before Kristyn beat him to it. He would have to tell her this week.

Whatever happened after that, he definitely wasn't going to Kristyn. How could he have been so stupid? To think she was the kind of girl he wanted to know.

But then, he used to be just like her.

❧

Liselle was fixing dinner when she heard the trusty garage door creak up. "I should probably get that oiled one of these days," she thought. "But then it is a great signal for when the kids come home."

She laughed quietly to herself. The kids were growing so fast. What would she and Tom do when they were gone?

"You're home early," she said with delight.

He smiled heavily.

"Yes, I'm tired. I'm going to bed right after dinner."

"Are you ill?"

"No, just a really rough day," he explained.

The week passed quickly and he was filled with dread every time he looked at Liselle, her beautiful hair pulled loosely off her face with the beginning platinum streaks. Her gentle blue eyes still reminded of sapphires; her once too-skinny frame now filled out. She was his beautiful mate and Proverb 18:22 played through his mind: *He who finds a wife, finds what is good and receives favor from the Lord.*

It was the little things, he realized, that he would miss, the way she held her coffee cup, the steam crinkling her eyes as she smiled at him. To never sit across from her again, the thought filled him with despair. Or when she planted a rosebush, watching her labor in the garden; activities that didn't appeal to him, yet defined who she was.

And the home she had created, the art reflecting the places they had visited, Mt. Vernon, the Caribbean and France, the light she brought to their home, to him.

It wasn't the little things; it was everything.

❧

Rising early one morning, his usual routine of being out the door before Liselle woke, he carefully searched for his Daily Prayer Book, a gift from the small parish church where he had grown up. He hadn't seen it in a long time and found it in the den, covered with dust and sadly neglected these many years. The heaviness remained as he slipped it in the pocket of his slacks.

At lunch he drove to a small park and got out of his car to walk the quiet paths. Stopping at a pond, he absently tossed pebbles in the water and restless he entered a quiet alcove where trees sheltered a weathered bench.

The aspens glowed brilliant yellow, their leaves diffused with sunlight and he caught his breath. Were they always this beautiful every autumn and he never noticed?

He sat on the bench and sobbed. Remembering the ancient book, he pulled it from his pocket where it fell open to a prayer by Augustine and slowly he began to read:

> "I came to love you late, O Beauty so ancient and new; I came to love you late. You were within me and I was outside where I rushed about wildly searching for you like some monster loose in your beautiful world. You were with me, but I was not with you. You called me, you shouted to me. You broke past my deafness. You bathed me in your light, you wrapped me in your splendor; you sent my blindness reeling. You gave out such a delightful fragrance, and I drew it in and came breathing hard after you. I tasted, and it made me hunger and thirst; you touched me, and I burned to know your peace."

The words tore at his heart. How did God know he would need them now? "God please help me. Forgive me, and forgive Kristyn, for being so blind to who you are and what's important. Please don't let me lose Liselle, I beg you, Lord God, Heavenly Father."

He had never prayed with such desperation, never felt such sorrow and raising his head to drink in the light he sensed God's peace, yet fear gripped his soul.

∾

Liselle could sense Tom's heaviness each evening and silently prayed that he would reach out to her and soon with whatever case was bothering him; what else could it be?

She stayed busy and involved with the kids' activities, the household duties. On Thursday he surprised her with plans for a weekend getaway. They would take the kids to Lucy's and go on to Whidbey Island for the weekend.

"I've never taken you there," he said.

∾

Liselle finished her last minute errands in record time. Traffic was light; she even had time to stop at the library. The day was glorious; she couldn't remember one quite so perfect or the peace that surrounded her now.

Walking to the car, she breathed deeply of the sweet air. Contentment, she had reached that plateau, and humming to herself she pressed the button to unlock the car door.

Pulling in the driveway, her heart felt light, their lives having knit together so beautifully. Surely no woman ever had a more perfect life. God was good and she sighed, anticipating the weekend with her husband.

Whidbey Island was as delightful as she remembered. They spent Saturday visiting gift shops and art galleries, found their favorite artist in one shop and spent the afternoon selecting a painting; arranging to have it shipped home. Liselle was excited about the art and the weekend it would celebrate.

That evening they dined in a small restaurant over a museum. The food was excellent but Tom was distant as he picked at his entree. She watched him quietly, hoping he would involve her, and soon, in whatever was consuming him.

"Tom," she said.

He looked up at her.

"What's wrong?"

"Nothing . . ."

"Come on Tom, I know you," she reminded him.

"Okay, everything is wrong."

Her heart did a little dance before it dipped into her shoes. "Is it us?" She asked.

"No, it's me," he said. "I haven't been honest with you all these years."

Again, her heart did that crazy little dance, this time up to her throat. She swallowed.

"You know, I've been on this island before," she began, trying to lighten the mood.

"You have, when?"

"This is where I came with the kids, when you went to Ivan's wedding," she said. "The girls got their little stuffed peacocks at a farm nearby."

"Oh," was all he said, toying with his half-empty wine glass. Was she stalling, trying to slow down his confession, did she suspect?

He paid the bill and they walked back to their room, hand in hand, quietly going through their bedtime routine, she beautiful in her negligee as they slipped into bed.

He held her in his arms and snuggled his head in her hair. Soon she felt her neck grow moist and hugging him tightly, she asked, "Why are you crying?"

"I've . . . I've been . . . unfaithful to you, to our marriage. I know you can never forgive me, but you are the only woman I've ever truly loved. I'm so sorry for what I've done. I would give anything to not have to confess this to you."

It seemed that her heart missed a beat. It couldn't be; it just couldn't.

"When, how, who?" she wanted to know all of it.

"Two law clerks, both young, trashy like me," he explained.

"Don't say that about you," she defended.

"It's true! What I did was trashy. It's too low for words. I didn't understand about God in my life back then, but that's a poor excuse for not keeping my marriage vows."

"Why now?" she asked, too shocked to pull away.

"Why am I telling you now," he repeated. "Because I'm about to be blackmailed by one of them; I never wanted to hurt you and if I could have those years back, they would be different."

She pulled away then and went into the bathroom, closed the door and turned on the ceiling fan to muffle her sobs in towels.

It was much later that she returned with swollen eyes.

He reached for her but she pushed his hand away.

"We'll talk in the morning."

Liselle slept exhausted, terrified to face the day and not wanting to wake to this new reality. It seemed that part of her had wept all night: dreaming or waking the pain was there.

Tom was stoking the fire and they looked at each other across the room as raindrops beat against the windows like bullets. "We needed some heat," he explained.

"Where do we go from here," she asked.

He came and sat beside her on the bed. "I don't want to lose all that we have, all that you mean to me, you're my life."

Pulling a small box from his pocket, he opened it to reveal a ring encircled with diamonds.

"Will you start over with me?"

She hadn't realized they needed to start over and holding out her hand, he slid the ring on her finger, the diamonds glittering in the fragile light.

"Because I would marry you all over," she repeated from an ad she once read.

He bent down to kiss her but she sat up, slipped on her robe and pulled her damp hair across one shoulder, settling in a chair by the fire.

"It will take time, Tom. This is not computing. We need a reset? Keep the eternity ring. I couldn't wear it right now. In fact, take my wedding ring, too. I can't believe you thought this could be fixed with . . . a ring? My vows meant something. I just want to know why?"

Fresh tears welled as he took the rings from her hand. "I don't know."

"You must have some idea; some stinking thinking that took you there."

His heart pounded as he drew air into his lungs and steeled himself.

"I was selfish. I was stupid. It was never about you. I guess I hated being in our home alone and I avoided being there."

"So anytime I left . . ." Liselle began.

"No! I'm not trying to put this on you. No!"

"Then keep going because I don't understand."

"I stayed out late when you were gone, then I got caught up in the whole sordid mess; it was easier to do than not do. That still sounds terrible, but I was incredibly selfish, only thinking of myself, feeling entitled."

"I get the picture but I don't accept it. If that's as deep as you can dig. I've heard enough," she finished.

"Whatever else you want to know," he promised.

Right now she wanted to be alone.

On the drive to Lucy's, Tom was struck at how they had traded places. His heart was now lighter for she hadn't said she would leave; while she had descended into darkness.

Still, he was apprehensive for she hadn't said she forgave, either.

Just before they reached Lucy's, she broke the silence.

"How are you planning to handle the law clerk?"

He reached for her hand.

"I'm just going to tell her that we worked it out," he explained.

"She won't be happy with that explanation. Who is it?"

"Kristyn," he mumbled.

"What? I thought you said Kristyn."

"I did," he confirmed.

"Wasn't she the one who called you at home a couple of times, when I had Henry?"

"I believe so," he again confirmed.

"My God, Tom, has this been going on that long?"

Incredulous she pulled her hand away.

"No, I swear. She left the firm shortly after Henry was born. I haven't seen her in all these years!"

"But you actually risked everything, our babies and their future happiness for some stupid law clerk!"

Now she felt like a fool. Her face flushed and her voice rose as the gloves came off.

"I can't believe you!"

No longer did she care what he thought for she had nothing left to lose. He had made a mockery of their marriage, the life she had assumed was hers, had narrowly escaped losing all these years now lay in dust at her feet, a skeleton of what she thought she had.

At Lucy's she was out of the car before it fully stopped and hurrying up the walkway to the kitchen. Greeting Lucy, she gathered the kids' bags.

"Did you have a good time?" Lucy asked.

"We had an interesting time," she answered as Tom followed her through the door.

28

TOM'S HEART WAS LIGHTER on Monday morning, Kristyn's ultimatum no longer frightening him. While he anticipated rough spots in working this out with Liselle, he was relieved and hopeful since she had not packed and left.

She had, however, remained moody and withdrawn. He would have to proceed with caution in these uncharted waters.

While Kristyn no longer had the power to destroy his marriage it was up to him to save it, and it was not going to be easy. Liselle's depression he could cope with, her anger he feared.

He was working through a stack of mail when Kristyn's call came.

"Hey, there Tom, ole' buddy, did you have a nice week?" she asked.

"Yeah, actually, it was pretty good!"

"So what's your answer?"

She was breathing heavily.

"Things are working out, we're staying together," he replied.

"Well, I don't believe you!" she exploded.

"Believe me, Kristyn, and my wife wants to meet you and tell you herself," he added.

There was a long silence.

"Kristyn . . . ?"

"Yeah, all right, I'll call your bluff! Where does she want to meet?"

"The Little Italy across from the law firm, you know where it is, 12:00 noon."

∽

It would be the most difficult meeting Liselle had endured, choosing the Little Italy for their meeting, once the catalyst for the life she now had.

How simple it had seemed so long ago when the meeting with Joseph Scudder was only to gain information about the cottage.

She had lain awake long after Tom fell asleep still numb from the shock that one she had trusted so completely could do such a devastating thing. It wasn't that he wasn't an attractive man. It was his dishonesty; the image of faithfulness he projected. How many lies had he told to maintain that façade?

Drifting off, the terrible reality came in her dream: *She and Tom were in bed when Kristyn joined them. Oblivious to Liselle, she began kissing Tom while he sheepishly acquiesced. Angry and shocked, Liselle moved to the guest room.*

She woke up; deeply disturbed and realized the truth she had tried to ignore. Tom had compartmentalized everything, even their marriage. For the first time she saw his true nature. After he had left St. Paul for college he never looked back, not even to invite his family to their wedding. She would never have ignored family that way and realized again how much she had lost with her parents' deaths.

Dozing off, the next time she woke, her stomach twisted in knots and she was filled with dread at the thought of facing this day. How raw the wounds, her life now hostage between love and anger; another lesson she would rather skip. What choice did she have? Early in life she had been forced to co-exist with pain.

Last night they talked about today's meeting, Liselle recalling their conversation as Tom stood before her, his eyes unfathomable in the lamplight, his words coming from deep anguish of soul.

"I've wasted my life on matters that weren't very important. I didn't understand what it meant to have the fruit of the Spirit in my life," he said. "The joy, peace, kindness, faithfulness, there's no law against those things, but I who practiced the law missed that truth. Love does no harm to its neighbor; love is the fulfillment of the law and yet I harmed you and my family. I've been reading the Proverbs of Solomon this past week," he continued.

"And all the wisdom is there, how to live life, how to avoid what I've done. I would give anything to do things differently, to let you know how important you are to me, and to serve the Lord with my whole heart for all of my life."

Though she didn't excuse his behavior, compassion flooded her and she reached for his hand, pulled him down beside her, his dark eyes filled with grief.

"Tom, this is the beginning, it's the trial run. We are finite people in a finite world but God wants to indwell and guide us!"

"I've accomplished so very little that is important," he responded.

"You have wonderful children; that was no accident! And we serve the God of second chances. I know he can restore the years you've lost; he did for me, but first you need to get right with God. Now is where it begins, not where it ends. Today is a part of eternity."

She paused to take deep breaths, last night's dream still heavy on her. "May I remind you what my father wrote me: 'What seems like a lifetime on earth is less than a millisecond in heaven so make it count.'"

$\sim$

Liselle was the first to arrive at the Little Italy and she had planned it that way. Requesting a table in the back, she sat with a view of the door while she waited for Tom and Kristyn to arrive.

Kristyn came first and Liselle watched her with curious interest as the waitress showed her to the table. Attractive in a cheap sort of way, the years had not been kind and sympathy flooded Liselle.

Without God in her life, she probably would have made the same bad choices, for her husband was an attractive man who pursued a materialistic life. Not that it was wrong to enjoy things, it was just wrong to put things before God and others.

She stood when Kristyn reached her.

"I'm Liselle Caribou," she greeted.

Thrown off guard, Kristyn slumped awkwardly into the chair across from her.

When Tom entered, Liselle glanced at him, her look admonishing him to keep silent. He sat down beside her and together they faced Kristyn, waiting until the waiter brought iced tea.

"Kristyn, I understand that you work in the legal profession . . ." Liselle began.

"Correct," she verified.

"Then you know that it is against the law to blackmail anyone."

"Well, sure, but . . ."

"I would prefer you keep your answers to 'yes' or 'no,'" Liselle interrupted.

"Yes," Kristyn replied.

"I know about your affair with my husband, you don't deny that?"

"No, but . . ."

"Again, no is sufficient!"

Kristyn glared at her. "No," she replied sullenly.

"Well, here's the deal, Kristyn. Blackmail is illegal. We all know about the affair. After this meeting, you will not bother my family or friends. This includes my husband, his co-workers, my children, my friends, and my family. This is your opportunity to say anything you want. After this, we will never hear from you again, is that understood?"

Liselle watched Kristyn's face change from arrogance to shock.

"Do you have anything to say?" Liselle asked.

"Why aren't you clawing my eyes out?"

"There's one thing I need to mention. As God forgave me, I forgive you," Liselle explained.

A guilty look crossed Kristyn's face before she snarled, "I do not need your forgiveness."

"No, of course you don't," Liselle agreed. "But someday . . . somehow . . . someway, I hope you realize your need for God's forgiveness. That's what matters."

Crossing her arms Liselle leaned back as Kristyn stared with unbridled hostility.

"If you have nothing to say, you may leave," Liselle admonished.

Kristyn scraped the floor with her chair as she pushed back and without a glance collected her handbag and retreated.

Liselle turned to face Tom as he sat hunched in his chair.

Cautiously he lifted his eyes. "You're amazing," he said.

At her silence, he continued: "I am so sorry for putting you through this. You don't deserve it and I will spend the rest of my life making it up to you."

She heard his words as a worthless IOU but knew that forgiveness was unconditional. It was the reconciliation that would be difficult.

"Please don't make me out to be a saint," she said. "I once read that *'forgiveness is the fragrance of the violet that clings to the heel of the one who crushed it.'* Christ was crushed for me and everywhere I go, I carry His fragrance. Perhaps I'm finally beginning to understand what forgiveness cost our Lord."

29

. . . they were but flesh, a passing breeze that does not return.

PSALM 78:39

LISELLE RETURNED HOME AND tried to stay busy, but a sense of unease hung over her, and a headache nagged. Tom's betrayal would sting for a very long time and she was not foolish enough to think that things could ever go back to the way they were or that the pain would ever completely leave.

She wasn't even sure she truly forgave him, for the adultery had struck at her core and who she believed they were as a couple. There was much work ahead if they were to salvage anything. How had it gotten so far off track? Had she been a terrible wife, unable to fathom his needs? Or was he really as selfish as he said?

She cringed at the thought that their intimate times had not been exclusive; that other women had shared such personal moments with her husband. Her husband's body belonged to her; she never consented to share it with another. Tom knew that about her; she thought they both had made that commitment on their wedding day.

The ache grew as she thought about their children. Could she really divorce Tom, even after his repentance? She didn't think she could, even though well-meaning friends spouted that divorce was her only option while others advised that she should have more self respect than to stay with an adulterous husband.

If she divorced, then what; find a new dad for her children, someone who may have done the same thing in his marriage? No, it seemed that the children were better off with both parents together. What well-meaning friends called "self-respect" seemed to her merely a shabby excuse for the ghastly pride that stalked them all.

Did Tom deserve grace? Did she? "Lord, I don't want to live this way!"

Filled with sadness, she went to sit on the terrace by the waterfall, feeling parched as she watched the cool water splashing over the rocks. It reminded of the psalm she had read that morning: "*All my fountains are in you.*" (87:7).

Jesus was the Living Water, the source of life and healing and she drew comfort knowing He was now beside her. A song came to mind: *I come to the garden alone, while the dew is still on the roses. And the Voice I hear as I tarry there . . .*

Her eyes feasted on the newly planted flowerbeds and she bent to pull a stray weed.

"Lord, is there a weed growing in my heart?"

Just like the DNA of a flower could not be changed by outside forces, so the Holy Spirit within would keep her true to His principles, unchanged by the bad acts of others.

She leaned against the sturdy oak, loving its strength and realized that perhaps she was no longer innocent to the ways of the world, but she could be true to peace and kindness.

Entering the kitchen, she heard the door bell and discovered the artwork from Whidbey being delivered. She carried the canvas to the garage, not ready to relive the day they had picked it out or the dreams shattered by Tom's confession.

～

That evening Tom skated around the edges of her emotions, offering to sleep in the guest room and give her space or comfort, whichever she needed.

She retired early and alone with an aspirin, her headache now a thundering freight train. She had dozed off when she heard the knock on her bedroom door and Claire stuck her head in.

"Claire what is it?"

"I just want to know why you're being so mean to Dad."

"How am I being mean to dad?"

"Kicking him out of your room, what's going on?"

"Your father and I have some issues to work out; you're too young to understand," Liselle explained, massaging her forehead.

"Why don't you try, mom, and not treat me like a baby."

"I'm sorry, Claire, not tonight!"

∾

The telephone erupted at 3:00 a.m. and she picked up on the second ring. Still in the twilight of sleep, she struggled to comprehend Geoff's words.

"I checked on Aunt Lucy . . . she wasn't breathing, must have dozed in her chair. Her heart; by the time paramedics . . ." His voice trailed off.

"I'll be there as soon as I can," she promised as grief folded her in half and hanging up she sobbed into her pillow; then padded down the hall to the guest room, opened the door.

"I'm awake, who was on the phone?" Tom asked.

"Geoff . . ."

"Great!" he exploded. "Why is he calling at this hour?"

"Lucy died," she said and walking back to the master suite, it hit her. What she perceived as Tom's jealousy of Geoff was really just his own insecurity. He didn't deserve further discussion right now, was not someone she trusted with her feelings. The revelation kept her awake and she prayed, "Lord, I still don't understand how he could do this?"

"Be still, my child. You were mine. Tom was not," the gentle Voice reminded.

∾

The kids slept late as she made phone calls to Lucy's attorneys and friends while Tom meekly did the breakfast dishes. She was on emotional thin ice and he a big part of the reason.

She tried to keep a strong front with the children when she told them, but that was never her style and tears flowed as Hank sobbed in her arms and the girls fled to their rooms.

She remained numb throughout the week, funeral arrangements keeping her busy, the loss of Lucy on top of Tom's betrayal now threatening to sink her. It seemed only yesterday that she had buried her mother. Was it really twenty years and another trusted confidante gone? Another terrible secret revealed?

God had given her Lucy before she realized her need of her. No one else had known her so well, or loved her so completely, except of course her mother. And she had loved both deeply; felt doubly blessed to have had two such extraordinary women in her life.

Like a switch being flipped on, she realized that everything they had loved had been passed on to her. She would see them again someday. She hadn't lost them; they just existed in another place.

30

Though you have made me see troubles,
many and bitter, you will restore my life again.

PSALM 71:20

THE FUNERAL WAS HELD in the little church on Anderson, attended by the islanders and many of Liselle's friends. It felt like someone had turned back the clock as the house filled with people and she mourned the woman who had been her best friend, once more facing a confession that begged for understanding.

Lunch at Lucy's mansion followed the burial. Now it all belonged to Liselle but it would always be Lucy's.

In the kitchen, Liselle poured herself iced tea, was squeezing lemon into her glass when she felt a tap on her shoulder. Turning, she stared into Geoff's face.

"Geoff, you startled me. I didn't hear you come in. Are you okay?"

He shrugged. "Who's going to live here now," he asked.

"Oh, the key," she said. "You still have that?"

"Yes, I can check on the house for you," he offered.

"I think it's best if I take it," she said. "Just to keep everything uncomplicated between us; you know what I mean."

His face fell as he reached in his pocket to retrieve it.

Tom left for Olympia after lunch, first reassuring Liselle that he would stay as long as she needed. But she was ready to be alone, had always healed best when alone with the still small voice of God.

She thought of her father who lost a son and wife; yet gained another wife and daughter. Her grandmother had lost her daughter; yet her two granddaughters had found each other. And she had lost her mother, yet found a cousin and a husband who had blessed her with a home and three children.

She felt inadequate to process Tom's betrayal. Was it worse than the other losses, harder maybe? She was older and should feel stronger. She didn't.

"Jesus, reduce me to love," she prayed.

While Claire, Chloe and Hank hung out around the estate, Liselle tackled Lucy's closet to pack away her clothes. Someone had told her to keep a few garments with special memories and when she came to the red velvet dress from their first Thanksgiving, the emerald taffeta from their first Christmas, she realized the value of their advice and carefully stored the two dresses in the cedar closet and on days when the loss seemed too great she would touch their softness and breathe in the fragrance that was Lucy.

After a week, the kids were ready to go back to Olympia. Early one morning Liselle drove them and spent the next two days filling the freezer with meals while she longed for the quiet of the island, longed to be alone to mourn Lucy.

On her final evening she explained her plans to Tom.

"I'm returning to Anderson tomorrow," she stated.

"Do you have more legal matters," he asked.

"No, all of the documents are pretty much in order. I just need some time by myself."

"How long will you be gone?"

"As long as it takes," she said. "I really don't know."

He looked at her uneasily. It was so unlike her to leave the kids for an extended period of time.

"I thought we were taking the kids to Alaska this summer," he began.

"The kids can go. I won't be able to, but you take them," she agreed.

He was stunned by her compliance. More than that, alarmed. This was not the reaction he had expected.

"Why are you acting so nonchalant about this," he inquired.

"Did I have anything to say about Lucy's passing, or your unfaithfulness?" she demanded. "No, I didn't. I'm not God, and I'm not in control of anything, am I?"

"Okay, peace!" he begged. "We'll discuss it in the morning."

She knew him too well, knew what he was thinking. If everything was all right between them, why wasn't she going? And she knew that everything was not all right. Not yet, not the way it should be for them to go on together.

～

In the morning she bustled around packing her new SUV, having traded her ancient car after Tom pointed out how unreliable it was for trips to Anderson.

"Call me if you need anything," she reminded the kids.

"Yes mother, for the umpteenth time," the girls said.

"So, I'm still taking the kids to Alaska," Tom inquired.

"Sure," Liselle agreed. "Hank will love it and they have cousins to hang out with."

～

As she headed north on the interstate, amazed at how fun the car was to drive, she set the GPS—not that she needed it—slid her cell phone into its cradle and turned up the volume from the steering wheel, adjusted the cruise control—again from the steering wheel—and moved the power seat forward.

With another touch of a button, the sun roof slid open and a cool breeze lifted her hair. Speeding along, she felt like royalty.

"Oh what a beautiful morning," she sang and on a whim, readjusted her GPS setting for Whidbey Island. It was crazy, she knew, she the responsible one, always there for the kids, now this impetuous decision. Why risk stirring up more painful memories.

～

The ferry delivered her with happy couples and lively children to the island and she had never felt more alone. Driving crowded streets, she spotted a vacancy sign at a hotel a block from the tourist shops and pulled in. Dropping the room key in her backpack, she wandered down to the beach where sun glinted on restless waves and steeled herself to visit the art gallery where they had shopped that day, Tom's words haunting her: "I would never do that to you."

How many times had he vowed his faithfulness?

She walked quickly through the gallery, "I'm just browsing," she greeted the clerk, relieved it was not the same one who had sold them the art.

Just a few steps away were the stairs to the restaurant above the museum. It didn't open until 5:00 but she ascended and gazed in the entrance. There was their table, near the window, set with linens and crystal for the next guests.

~

She spent a restless night in the lonely bed, tossing and turning, never asleep long enough to dream; Tom's early morning call waking her.

"Hey, we're leaving this morning, beautiful," he greeted. "You didn't tell me when you're coming home?"

Still the controller, this time the brakes came off her anger and her voice rose.

"I'm on Whidbey."

There was a long silence on the line.

"With Geoff," he asked.

"Is that what you think of me? Do you remember our weekend, Tom, or was it just another adventure for you?"

"I wouldn't blame you . . ." he began.

She hung up, showered and packed, loaded her car and headed for the ferry. The drive from Mukilteo was uneventful as she drank a smoothie, munched a power bar and mulled over her foray to Whidbey. What had she accomplished except to remind of loss?

Maneuvering her car from the ferry at Anderson, soon she was turning into the driveway of the old mansion and pulling up to the carriage house with its tiny windowed attic.

Parking inside, she wondered why she had never thought to explore the attic. When Lucy was alive the main house had seen all the activity. It had never occurred to them that anything of interest could be in the carriage house.

Having stopped for food, she carried the bags inside and sat at the kitchen counter for a quick meal, the silence real and the memories haunting, Lucy, Tom, Christmas with the kids brought tears and smiles. God's love was sometimes subtle but now it overwhelmed her with the memories of Hank asleep on her shoulder, the first time she held her baby girls.

"Lord, if I don't resolve this, it will tarnish my children forever," she said.

~

She retired early that night, snug in grandmother's room, as unchanged, cozy and welcoming as ever and refused to worry about the kids. Whatever will be, will be, she reminded herself . . . *que sera, sera*. How had her father survived the loss of a child? She was sure she could never survive such and pulling out her Bible, she quickly breathed a prayer of safety for her children.

She remembered God's promise to bless her and not harm her, as the prophet Jeremiah had written long ago. However far God wanted to take her to teach her humility, she would follow for He would never betray her.

Turning to a passage in Ecclesiastes, she read until she dozed off.

"There is a time for everything, and a season for every activity under heaven . . . a time to be born and a time to die . . . a time to weep and a time to laugh, a time to mourn and a time to dance."

3 1

THE EARLY MORNING LIGHT woke her and she drew grandmother's goose-down comforter around her to ward off the chill. How close had she come to losing the man she loved to another woman? Would she ever be able to trust him again?

Thoughts of Tom stroked her mind and the reminder that one mistake in youth could haunt you for the rest of your life.

She picked up her Bible where it lay and continued to read: *"A time to keep and a time to throw away, a time to tear and a time to mend, a time to be silent and a time to speak."*

What season was she in, a time to tear and throw away?

Again her thoughts swung to her children. "Thank you Lord, for my children; protect them."

She heard the doorbell chime.

No one knew she was here and alarmed she swung her feet into slippers, grabbed her robe and padded down the hallway.

Peeking out the stained glass window she could just make out a shadowy shape, slim, tall; blond.

Geoff leaned with his face pressed against the frosted glass peering in and she crouched down; thankful her car was in the carriage house with no windows; doubly thankful that she had retrieved the key from him.

Waiting, holding her breath, she counted the persistent rings, two, three, four more times and breathed a sigh of relief when he finally got in his car and drove away.

It was unlikely anyone else would stop today. It was also unlikely she would ever consider a tryst with him. How easy it had been for Tom, because she gave him freedom, had trusted him?

～

She dressed, made toast and tea and tucked her hair up under a baseball cap. Tears welled at the sudden memory of Lucy telling her to cover her hair before they went into the attic.

"Miss Gorgeous," she had called her.

Crunching across the gravel to the carriage house, she climbed the stairway to the dusty attic where a lone ray of sunshine shone through the grimy window. As she suspected, the attic had no lights and she retrieved a flashlight from her car. Switching it on, dust bunnies stirred.

It took a moment for her eyes to adjust and she shuddered at the cobwebs, old dress forms and furniture shrouded in sheets. A mouse scurried past as she scanned the space. Where to start?

Her eyes strayed to a leather strap jutting up from the floor and on closer inspection she could see the outline of a trapdoor. Kneeling, praying that nothing jumped out at her, she tugged on the handle; losing her balance as the leather disintegrated in her hand.

Searching through the tool box, she selected a metal file and inserted it under the edge to pry up the door. Inside the opening between the rafters lay a tattered blanket wrapped around a bundle of letters. Placing a hand over her heart, she took a deep breath before carefully lifting the bundle and hurrying down the stairs to the kitchen.

On the counter she pulled the layers apart as brittle newspaper and yellowed letters threatened to crumble. The first article was the newspaper report that Lucy had found all those years ago, this one a bit more specific:

Steilacoom General: Baby girl *it read, born March 20, 1926 to E. Cottington.*

She examined the rest of the faded letters addressed to grandmother from Jos Vanderhorst of Holland, the handwriting in imperfect English.

Dear Elizabeth,
March 26, 1926

I sorry for delay in write, spend seven months prepare place for you. I wait you. Please no impatient, love, everything ok.

Forever,
Jos

So Jos was Grandmother's lover, the phantom grandfather she never knew. The letter was confusing for Ellen had been born six days before the letter was written, adopted before the letter was delivered. Did Jos not know that Elizabeth was pregnant? Apparently not, since he mentioned seven months had passed. The next letter was postmarked from India.

> *Dear Elizabeth,*
> *June 22, 1929*
>
> *Writing every week from many place. You upset I go. I want us to-gether. I beg you write. In December I bring you Holland.*
>
> *Forever,*
> *Jos*

Definitely a mix-up; by then grandmother had married Captain and was pregnant with Lucy's father, apparently never receiving the other letters from Jos.

At the bottom of the stack was one last note in Grandmother's handwriting.

> *Dear Lord, I don't know why I lost my daughter, but you know what's best. I pray your protection over her and the lives of those who will love her. May she find the happiness she deserves and serve you with her whole heart.*

Liselle placed the letters back in the worn envelopes as sadness engulfed her. Grandmother's prayer had certainly been answered and now she knew what happened, had a name and place for a grandfather long dead, the final chapter in her search.

A wave of sorrow washed over her, surprising her with its intensity, like the moment Tom had confessed his adultery and nothing was ever the same again, the familiar once again evaporating to be replaced with questions and vulnerabilities and a new course to be charted.

"Would it always be this hard, Lord?"

She hadn't told Lucy about the adultery but she could hear her now, knew what she would say: how can you even think of tearing the children away from their father and upending their lives?

And Lucy would be right for just last week another friend had announced her divorce and her children had spiraled into confusion. Over the years, she had watched divorced friends and their children struggle to make sense of crumbling homes that had seemed rock solid *like hers*.

She had only to look at statistics to know the odds were against her children surviving such trauma without emotional scars. It had been difficult enough for her not having a dad around. But her son! She couldn't do it; yet when she looked at Tom, she felt only anger, disappointment.

Would she really risk destroying her children just to salvage her pride? She knew the answer but it was hard to accept, for pride had risen like a genie long held captive and suddenly released from its bottle. In that moment she realized once you gave in to sin, it had its hook in you, whether it was anger, lust, arrogance or deceit.

"Jesus, how did you love so much?"

She bowed her head; knowing she hadn't reached forgiveness yet. "Forgive me, Lord, for all the times I've sinned against you," she prayed.

It would take time for her to heal, for Tom, too, the thought new for her. While she had the pain, he had the guilt but the hardest part was the lies. Adultery was one thing, but layered over that was his continuous vow that he would never do it *when he was.*

≈

Liselle spent the next day reading by the pond before walking to her cottage. The kids had long since abandoned any interest in the garden and she had sown wildflowers along the creek bank.

If a seed falls on good ground, it will bear much fruit, she thought of Christ teaching his disciples in Luke 8:8. How true of Lucy who in turn planted many seed in other lives.

She sat in the sun beside the lonely stilt now covered in flowers and closed her eyes as tears streamed down her face.

When she opened them, Geoff sat crouched before her.

"This is where I rescued you last time, remember, beside this stilt?" he asked softly.

"Oh, Geoff, why are you here?"

"You need to consider what I have to offer, Liselle, I would never leave you alone."

"Geoff, you can't keep doing this to me," she replied.

≈

She went to the little church on Sunday but it proved too traumatic, the pain of the adultery too raw. As the congregation stood to sing of God's love, a deep sob rose in her chest and broke in her throat. She sobbed without tears, without sound, her pain beyond any she had ever experienced, beyond the loss of mother and Lucy.

Abruptly she left the service while those nearby gave knowing looks. "How much she loved Lucy," they said.

Later that afternoon, seeking the pastor's advice, he listened as she explained her struggle. "Wasn't I attractive enough? Couldn't Tom just say no and walk away? I never considered an involvement with another man; my marriage was my life!"

"Liselle, it's not about being attractive," the wise man explained. "And there's never an excuse for adultery; none!"

He was empathic on that point.

"I want you to stop looking for blame anywhere but on Tom. The sin rests squarely on him. It was his choice, for whatever reason and not anything anyone else did."

∾

The nights were hardest, lying in bed reviewing all the pain, the losses, and the times when Tom had taken her for granted. Wallowing in pity, she became depressed. Tom and Lucy had been her closest confidantes, the only ones she had trusted so completely. Lucy was dead and Tom had betrayed her. She felt all alone again, the way she had when mother died.

"*I promised never to leave you,*" the Voice reminded. "Thank you, Lord," she breathed.

∾

Settling into bed one night, she knew she was losing the battle to heal. "*Do you want to be right? Or do you want to be happy?*" Mother had asked her long ago when she didn't want to forgive a friend's mistake. And mother was right; being apart from Tom now gave her no satisfaction, the reality of his long ago transgression not relevant to where they were.

"Help me, Lord, I'm floundering here," she prayed and opening her Bible to Psalm 4, she began to read, "You know that the Lord has chosen for himself those who are loyal to him. The Lord listens when I pray to him. When you are angry, do not sin. Think about these things quietly as you go to bed. Do what is right as a sacrifice to the Lord and trust the Lord."

It was a watershed moment, the challenge before her great, the complexity and scope of the words striking her in a way she had not seen before; the answer of how to deal with her marriage—do what's right! She might always have a scab on her heart, but she could go forward because she didn't like her other options.

181

The pain was impossible to ignore, but the Lord was showing her a different path from those opinions freely offered her. Repentance and reconciliation were the heart of God. He was the Great Restorer of all that was broken.

Tom had put down good roots in the soil of love and kindness. Faithfully he had worked for his family over the years, and after his youthful indiscretions, when it would have been easy to pursue the many temptations that seduced a bright young attorney full of passion and a lucrative future, he had chosen the high road and left the other women behind.

He didn't deserve any medals for that; but he had changed, and that counted with God for forgiveness, like love, was a choice. She loved Tom, wasn't finished with the idea of "us". And she knew he loved God; she could tell by his actions. His heart had changed.

Now she thought of Grandmother's loss, her mistake causing her to lose her baby girl followed by the loneliness of being a young widow. The secret to survival was to forgive and live life. That's what father had written so long ago, make life count.

Her heart swelled with love for the man who had given her life.

32

THE NEXT MORNING, SHE knew it was time to go home, time to rejoin her life and to sacrifice her "right" to a perfect marriage. Marriage didn't come that way Lucy had tried to tell her so long ago when Hank was born.

It was time to rebuild, to put flesh and blood on the skeleton that lay at her feet.

With hope she packed her car and locked Lucy's mansion, savoring her last moments of quiet. Tom and the kids would be back from Alaska this evening and she would have dinner ready.

Backing down the driveway, she glanced in her rearview mirror. A sport car was pulling in behind her and she slammed on the brakes.

Geoff jumped out and hurried up the driveway.

Powering down her window, she stuck out her head.

"Anything wrong, Geoff?"

"Oh, Liselle, it's you! I didn't recognize the car!"

"Yeah, I finally traded in the old."

"It's about time, with Tom driving the fancy Euros. What brings you here?"

"Nothing, really," she explained. "Just checking on things . . ."

"All you have to do is call, we're neighbors and I'm here regularly. I can keep an eye on the place for you."

"Why are you here so often?"

"I'm moving back, be the rich little island boy!"

"Well, good luck on that one, I've really got to run," she explained.

"How about lunch . . ."

"Thank you but I've really got to get going."

She put the car in reverse as he placed his hand on her door. Hitting the power locks, she powered up her window.

"C'mon Liselle!" he hollered as she eased down the driveway.

"No thank you, Geoff, now please remove your hand and your car!"

He dropped his hand and slouched back to his car, but to her astonishment, he began to pull forward closing the gap between them.

Glancing around, she spotted an opening in the hedge and cranking the wheel hard right she lurched through the opening, circled across the lawn, and plowed through the hedge behind him.

His stunned look was the last thing she saw in her mirror as she hit the gravel driveway and churned rocks in his direction.

Back in Olympia, she pulled into a car wash to check the damage to the car; then stopped at a card shop.

She needed to make an effort with Tom. She knew he was in limbo; for once in his life, he didn't know how to proceed.

Selecting a card she returned to her car and pulled it from the bag to read one more time:

You are my life and without you, I'd still be looking for happiness.

The words sang *truth* and she wouldn't change any of them. Sighing, she slipped the card in its wrapper. One thing she was certain of: Tom had changed her life in good ways and given her the future she wanted.

Along the way he had made poor choices, paid a price she would never know, but he had grown, was now truly faithful to her and God. That had to count in the plan of forgiveness—second chances—for she knew deep in her soul that he was committed to their marriage.

～

Already back from Alaska, Tom walked into the kitchen as she was fixing dinner. "Looks like you hit something with your car," he stated.

"Oh, I did bump the hedge at Lucy's house," she explained.

"It looks like you 'bumped' it pretty hard!"

"Do I need to call the insurance?" she asked.

"Might be a good idea to have it repainted, you don't want it to get rusty."

～

After dinner and the kids disappeared to their rooms, she gazed at Tom as they sat in the den and the silence stretched out between them.

"I'm glad you had a good time with your family," she offered.

"It was good for the kids to finally see my childhood home," he agreed.

"Well, judging by their comments at dinner, it was a positive experience."

"Yes. How was your time on Anderson?"

"It was very worthwhile. I needed that time to get my head together, to try and understand the unexpected turns that life has taken. I sometimes think I never properly grieved my mother, moving to Anderson so quickly and all the changes that came. Lucy's passing seemed to reopen all that pain," she explained.

"And did you come to any conclusion about us," he asked.

"It became clear to me that God preserved our marriage. At any other time, had you told me about the affairs, or had I found out by chance, I would have left you in a heartbeat, totally unable to deal with the whole concept of that degree of betrayal or forgiveness. But God has shown me the truth this week, that every sin is awful, from pride to adultery. And He forgives it all. I must learn to do the same."

He knelt before her then and placed his hands on her knees.

"You are my treasure, you know that, don't you?" he asked, his dark eyes glowing. "I've never told you this," he confessed, "but whenever you're away is still my worst time. I'm afraid that someday you will leave me."

A deep pang pierced her heart. "I had no idea," she said.

"I know," he agreed. "Those are my demons to work out. Before, I chose the very worst way. The adultery had nothing to do with you, with us, but all those feelings came back today when I thought I was coming home to a house without you."

Tears came to her eyes as she gazed at the man before her.

"Was this really going to be a sacrifice, Lord?" It seemed that the answer to the question, to the man gently holding her, was obvious.

"You're the only man I ever wanted . . ."

"It would serve me right if you did love someone else . . ." he began.

"Don't even think that way, it isn't possible."

She put her arms around him and kissed him.

"You're the only man I could ever love and that ring you gave me on our wedding day, I will wear it now with the eternity ring."

$\sim$

That evening, preparing for bed, she heard Tom coming up the stairs and met him at the door. A question remained in his eyes.

She smiled and took his hand. "I have something to show you."

She led him to the wall opposite their bed where she had hung the art they bought on Whidbey that day.

"A reminder to both of us," she explained. "Our God forgives everything and everyone. There is none among us who can boast we don't need it."

He buried his head in her hair and sobs rose in his throat.

Overcome by his sorrow and their collateral pain, her tears joined his. After all the years and missed cues, true intimacy had come. She loved him more than the day they had married, with a love that only God could give.

Tom was a man after God's heart and if she had in any way been a part of his transformation, she was grateful for the journey.

> *Be at rest once more, O my soul, for the Lord has been good to you. For you, O Lord, have delivered my soul from death, my eyes from tears, my feet from stumbling, that I may walk before the Lord in the land of the living.* Psalm 116

Epilogue

How can I repay the Lord for all his goodness to me?

PSALM 116:12

HER FIRST CHRISTMAS WITHOUT Lucy, Liselle approached the holidays with trepidation, her loss sharp as she carried boxes of ornaments to the front room and paused to study the perfectly shaped tree.

The scent of pine filled the room to stir memories of the island where she and Lucy had met, or more accurately, connected; cousins who hadn't known of each other until the spring Ellen had died.

The first box of ornaments belonged to Lucy; filled with exquisite carved nativity figures and hand-blown glass wonders from Grandmother's Victorian collection. Touching them, Liselle felt a thread connecting her to those who were gone.

She finished decorating the tree and went upstairs to dress for dinner. It was their twenty-fourth Christmas together and Tom was taking her someplace special. Selecting an emerald green sweater, tweed slacks and her favorite suede boots, she reached in her jewelry case for her pearls.

As she did, she noticed the two halves of the heart necklace, the E on each one clearly visible. As she picked them up, they dangled from her fingers like two wind chimes in a breeze, reminding her of Lucy and the love she had given, the pleasure she had taken in family.

She thought of her daughters, as different as she and Lucy had been, yet as closely bound together. In a flash she knew what she must do.

~

Claire and Chloe resided on campus at the University of Washington and arrived early on Christmas morning. Liselle laughed as they swooped in to kiss her before joining Hank in the kitchen where he wolfed down pancakes.

Tom was lazy this morning and Liselle savored her time with the kids.

"This is for you," she said, handing each daughter a narrow black box.

Claire popped hers open first. "Old jewelry mother—really?"

Curious, Chloe opened hers and lifted the necklace. The E she was familiar with; mother had worn it for years, as had 'Aunt' Lucy. She turned it over and on the back was a newly engraved C.

"Claire, don't be such a dork," she said. "Look at the back!"

"Sorry, mother," Claire said, familiar with the pendants' history.

"You're too much like me, Claire."

Liselle smiled as Claire rolled her eyes and Tom appeared in robe and slippers.

"Do I smell pancakes," he inquired as the girls fastened their necklaces and Liselle poured his coffee. He raised an eyebrow at her and she shook her head.

How well they knew each other—the signal passing between them like ships in a rough sea. And Tom's betrayal had been a rough sea, but along the way Liselle had learned that God was their refuge, underneath His everlasting arms of love.

The scope of Psalm 139 reached her now: "Where can I go from your Spirit?"

She knew the answer to that question. Placing the steaming mug before Tom, he caught her hand in his.

"Thank you," he said, kissing her palm.

www.ingramcontent.com/pod-product-compliance
Lightning Source LLC
Chambersburg PA
CBHW072355030726
47505CB00014B/1843